At the age of thirty-eight, Inga Olafson thought she'd never find happiness again. Her wealthy and powerful ex-husband had traded her in for two girls half her age, and she thought that all was lost. But then the wealthy and powerful Caleb Essex entered her life and reintroduced her into the world of limitless sensuality. And when the young, inexperience, and wickedly curious corporate assistant, Maggie, enters into their life, passion explodes like never before. Meanwhile, their coworker, Kimberly, discovers a whole new world of passion with the other executives in the office, Bryce and Adam, and discovers that men in pairs can be something more than just twice as fun. But in a world like Golden Valley, Montana during the gold rush, keeping secrets—like a menage romance—is both critical and nearly impossible. Kimberly risks everything for the love that she has always ached for.

The Wicked, Wild West

ISBN: 978-1-4874-3937-8
Cover art by Angela Waters

Published by Extasy Books Inc

Look for us online at:
www.extasybooks.com

The Wicked, Wild West

By

Robin Gideon

Dedication

This one is dedicated to Keith.

CHAPTER ONE

Golden Valley, Montana

Inga Olafson looked at the clock on the office wall—the big one that chimed on the hour and had Roman numerals—and felt a certain sense of dread go through her. It was almost ten minutes past eight, and Kimberly Case still wasn't at her desk. And Inga knew that Kimberly had been warned that there would be consequences—whatever that meant—if she was late for work again. In a goldrush city like Golden Valley, premiere jobs for women were coveted—and Kimberly had one of them.

Inga didn't really know Kimberly that well. Kimberly had started with the Cattleman's Emporium Saloon and Casino, one of the largest corporations in the territory two months earlier, and Inga had been there only three months herself. But during the times that they could converse privately and personally, she had gotten to know Kimberly, and liked her.

So why, when she seemed like such a sensible woman, was Kimberly consistently showing up late for work?

She's got a good job with bosses who pay her well and treat her with dignity, she thought. *She's sabotaging herself. Why in hell would she do that?*

She glanced over at Margaret *Maggie* Williams, the newest of the three secretaries working for the top executives of Golden Valley's most prestigious company, Cattleman's Emporium Corporation. The girl—and at eighteen Maggie was really just a girl—was studiously reading the reports that had come to the telegraph office during the previous evening hours.

I wish Kimberly took her duties as seriously as Maggie does, Inga thought, then shook her head a little, and tried to put her concerns away where they wouldn't plague her thoughts. She had enough concerns on her plate just seeing to it that Caleb Essex was pleased with the work that she did for him. She had her own life and her own boss to concern herself with. Caleb was more than enough man to keep a secretary busy.

As though he could read her mind, his office door, directly behind Inga, opened and Caleb stuck his head into the outer office.

"Miss Inga, could I please have my morning coffee now?"

When she looked at him, her heart skipped a beat. It always did that whenever she looked at him, particularly when it was first thing in the morning. He was, without question, the most handsome man she had ever seen. And since she was thirty-eight and a divorcee, it wasn't as though she was a blushing ingénue new to the game of amour.

But, as she reminded herself, she might not be thinking entirely rational, entirely reasonably. When a passionate woman—and she most certainly was that—went two full years without making love, her thoughts and emotions were not necessarily at their most lucid.

Has it really been over two years? she asked herself. *Yes, of course it has,* she almost immediately answered her own question. *You were thirty-six when your husband traded you in for two girls half your age. He hadn't touched you long before he left you, and yet he got both of those girls pregnant at the same time. It hasn't been two years—it's been closer to three pushing on four.*

Closing her eyes, she felt impotent rage begin rising within her. Yes, her husband had traded in a thirty-six-year-old wife for two eighteen-year-old pregnant mistresses. But he had power in St. Louis, and he could destroy her—so he did. Because he could. And bastards like that did things like that.

"Inga," Maggie said softly, breaking into her troubled thoughts, "Mr. Caleb asked you for his coffee."

Inga gave the girl a grateful look and said, "Thank you. Sometimes I can be so addle-brained, and he does so hate it when it takes me too much time to do what he asks of me."

"You'll have to teach me what he likes," the girl said quietly. "Promise me you will? That way I can help you to make him happy."

Inga nodded as she got out of her chair and hurried to the door. The main floor of the building was divided into sections, each catering to a customer's specific wishes—provided they had the money to afford the high quality but high-priced goods that the Cattleman's Emporium Saloon and Casino was selling. The main section was a casino and saloon, which was clearly what attracted most of the clientele. A second, though certainly smaller section, was a quiet restaurant. The third section, dimly lighted at all times, was an intimate tavern where words between men and women were always softly spoken.

This last section was the only place where women who didn't work for the establishment were allowed.

She got the daily pot of coffee for Caleb from the kitchen on the main floor, then hurried back up to the second-floor executive offices.

She picked up the coffee pot from the table, then poured a cup. Then, with her back to Maggie, she unbuttoned the top button of her blouse. She still wasn't showing much of her extravagant bosom, but she was showing more of her cleavage than she was when he had first started working for Caleb.

On more than just a few occasions, she had caught him looking at her breasts. This pleased her on several levels. The first was that she liked it when he looked at her and was clearly taking masculine pleasure in her feminine charms. The second was that he looked at her without ogling her. To be looked at was to be appreciated; to be stared at was to be crudely lusted after.

The difference between the two was as different as day is from night.

She knocked on the door lightly three times, just like she did every morning at this time. After a moment she heard Caleb say, "Come in, Inga."

She felt a certain sense of relief in that Caleb seemed in a good mood. With the price of gold fluctuating the way it was lately, his temperament could be mercurial, sometimes ecstatic with the way the market was rising, and at other times utterly quiet and sullen as he worried about forces he often had no control over which were moving in a direction he did not want to think too long on.

Inga paused for a moment, coffee cup and saucer in hand, before she stepped into the office.

He was sitting behind his desk when she entered the room and was reading the telegraphs that had come in during the night. His black cotton suit had been hand-sewn by the finest tailors in Golden Valley, Eli and Susan Smythe. The garment had cost a small fortune and looked it. Caleb's hair was cut once a week. He had prematurely gray hair now at the temples—which only made him more handsome in Inga's eyes. He was a man who was aging with the grace of a Roman god.

There wasn't anything about Caleb that she didn't find visually delicious.

She hadn't tasted him, but that didn't stop her from imagining what a scrumptious meal he might make.

And since she had gone more than two years without sex—and much longer than that without *satisfying* sex—her taste buds were on alert. So was her clit.

A shiver went through her, but she didn't let it show. Since she'd begun working for Caleb, she'd learned to hide her body's reactions to him. It was important to do that, she understood. But doing it wasn't easy or comfortable.

Without saying a word, she walked across the room, stepping lightly around the large and brightly polished mahogany desk, and set the cup and saucer on the desk in front of him. She always tried not to say anything until he spoke to her first. She didn't want to disturb his concentration. Her respect for the man she worked for bordered on idolatry, and though she suspected such an emotion probably wasn't very healthy, she knew it was true, and she was making no effort to change her opinion.

"Thank you, Inga," Caleb said when she set his coffee down. She was standing near his elbow. Though he was not looking up at her, she could feel his presence to the marrow of her bones. He said, "Tell me, what do you think of this?"

Inga's heart skipped yet another beat when he pointed at a sentence in the telegram he was reading. In the three months that she had been working for him, he'd often asked for her opinion, but it was never about a business matter. It was always about something that was inconsequential, something that wasn't critically important. This time he was including her in his business life—and that made all the difference in the world. She was aware that she had just been invited into a more important part of Caleb's life.

The realization thrilled her.

She had to read the sentence three times before her brain was functioning properly enough to make sense of the words. It was about a railroad route change, and whether or not Caleb—and his company—would allow it. She read it one more time.

"Yes," she said after a moment, "I'd agree to it, and I wouldn't ask for additional transportation fees, either." She cleared her throat nervously and wished that her Swedish accent was less pronounced. She was always a little embarrassed by her accent, though she knew she shouldn't be. Caleb had said that it pleased him.

"Not ask for more money?" Caleb's eyes narrowed as he looked up at her. "Why not?"

Caleb was a man comfortable with demanding more money. He always kept his eyes on the profit line.

"You're going to make more money because the new route will take less time," she said, though now she was consciously aware of how her thigh, as she stood, was touching Caleb's thigh while he sat in his chair. To her, it seemed to be a shockingly intimate caress, though logic and reason told her it was only the casual contact of a secretary working with her employer. "If you ask for more money, they're going to resent it. But if you don't ask for more money, they'll think they're getting something for nothing, while you'll know that you're making more money, no matter what. Let them think they've gotten the better of you, but you'll know you've turned a nice profit."

Caleb smiled up into her eyes, and she'd never seen such a lovely smile in her life. It wasn't just her heart that responded—it was other parts of her, like her nipples and her labia and most of all her clit that paid rather particular attention to Caleb's admiration.

Caleb turned in his chair so that he more directly faced her, and she was now standing between his wide-spread knees. His smile had changed subtly. It had transformed from being delightfully charming to being roguishly seductive. Every one of her feminine senses was aware of the difference.

Especially her clit.

It was always her clit that first noticed the change in Caleb's mood. Always.

"How did such a woman as yourself become so wise in the ways of business?" he asked. "And how is it that the American business world hasn't picked up on this? I feel astoundingly lucky to have you in my employ."

Inga shrugged her shoulders, and when she did, her significantly-more-than-ample bosom wiggled and swayed within the confines of a chemise that she had hoped would not allow attention-getting movement. To that extent, the chemise was an abysmal failure. Inga suddenly wished she had worn a corset that morning, which she almost always did. She always had to do what she could to keep her voluptuousness harnessed.

With Caleb sitting and her standing, her breasts were ominously or fortuitously at face-level to Caleb, a fact which she was intensely aware of.

It was always her breasts which drew the most attention from men. Sometimes she liked the fact and sometimes she didn't, but at the age of thirty-eight she had learned to accept her body for what it was.

"Will there be anything else, sir?" she asked, the tension in her voice so tight she couldn't possibly hide it. Nervousness also seemed to make her Swedish accent more prominent. "Is there anything more I can do for you?"

She immediately wished she hadn't spoken the last words. There was something distinctly submissive in them. She looked into Caleb's eyes, and she saw the sexual tension there. She felt her sex tighten and moisten and knew with a woman's certainty that she needed to escape. She needed to run away as fast and far as she could, because if she didn't then only bad things could and would happen. She understood this instinctively, as only a woman could.

Men could never understand such truths. Their brains just didn't work that way.

"You probably want to get back to work," she heard herself say. In her ears, the words sounded strange, as though someone else had spoken them.

She felt as though she was suddenly in someone else's body.

Before she got to the door, Caleb was directly behind her. She could feel the heat of his body so close to her that she could hear his rapid breathing. When he put his palms flat on the door, surrounding her with his arms without actually touching her, she suddenly felt as though she was a captive to his power, his charisma, his intense virility. The awareness was as exhilarating as it was terrifying.

"Do you really need to leave?" His lips were so close to her ear that she could feel the heat of his breath as he spoke. As never before in her life, she suspected herself to be on the verge of a climax.

Seconds passed before she finally answered, "No. But I should."

"But you don't want to, do you?" His voice invisibly caressed intimate places on her body. And everywhere his voice touched, she responded.

Inga's eyes were closed when she silently answered his question by giving her head a little shake. Caleb closed the distance that separated them so that his chest pressed against her back. When she was aware of the contact, she gasped softly. Her arms folded, and then she was fully pushed against the door, her cheek and breasts pressed against the hard surface, with his solid chest against her back—and his pelvis, which was now sporting a significant bulge, pressed against the globes of her ass. He moved his hips from side to side, and she could feel his excitement. His erection was formidable.

Did he want her . . . back there? The thought made a shiver go through her. The possibility was filled with mystery . . . and frightening anticipation.

"Caleb," she said softly, her cheek and breasts against the door, her heart pounding against her ribs, "I . . . I . . ."

She knew there were words that needed to be spoken, but she couldn't think of what those words should be. Should she beg that he not stop until she finally—at long last—achieved the sexual satisfaction that had eluded her for her entire life? Her better judgment and her body's needs were at war. She wanted to think lucidly and rationally, but desire wouldn't let her.

He kissed her temple, then kissed her cheek and she felt herself getting wetter, getting more creamy by the second. In her entire life she had never reacted so wantonly to a man, and for her to do it now was both magical and mysterious. She could feel the pulse of her heart in her clit, and the sensation this caused gave her something akin to a sense of wonder.

Things like this don't happen to me, she thought.

Her next thought was, *Yes they do . . . when you're with Caleb.*

She felt her nipples tighten and she pressed her breasts just a little more firmly against the door. She could feel Caleb's breath against the side of her face, and even more evocatively, could feel the solidity of his erection against the cheeks of her bottom as he moved his hips from side to side. He seemed very large. The awareness was wickedly arousing, though she suspected it shouldn't be.

The thought that he might want to take her Greek-fashion once again slithered through her consciousness, and once again she shivered. Even though she could only judge the man by what she felt as he rubbed against her, he seemed significantly larger than the only man she was familiar with.

Actually, he seemed much, much more than her body had ever had to accommodate.

And the thought of taking him anally was altogether frightening. And exciting. Caleb elicited nothing but extremes . . . and she adored him because of it.

"You've bewitched me," he whispered hotly into her ear. "I think about you day and night." She heard him sigh and felt his breath on her cheek. "I never mix work with pleasure. Never."

She felt his hands go from her hips up her ribs, and then slide forward to move over her breasts. He caressed her firmly, commandingly, his fingers buried into her covetously. He was a man who was taking his pleasure, not begging for it. Everything about him made her tremble with desire.

She whispered a word she wished she hadn't, since she didn't like to blaspheme, but once she'd said it, she repeated the word several times in rapid succession. Caleb seemed to know precisely how to squeeze her nipples through her clothing, using just the right amount of pressure to draw the absolute amount of pleasure from her.

"You intoxicate me," he said, his breath warm against her ear as he spoke. "I've tried to stay away from you, but I can't. I simply can't."

She doubted he could have spoken more seductive words. There wasn't a single cell in her body that didn't respond favorably to what he'd just said.

He pressed himself more firmly against her and she felt herself to be on the brink of a climax that was different than any she'd ever before experienced. She'd always provided her own orgasms, and even then it usually only happened after quite a while of manual stimulation and serious, concerted effort to achieve the desired result. But with Caleb, she found herself almost frighteningly close to orgasm at the first look he gave her, at the first touch of his body against hers.

How can that be? she asked herself. *It's always been so difficult to climax, and I've always had to cause them myself.*

She suspected then that Caleb possessed magical powers, possibly even demonic powers. How else could a mere mortal man have such control of her body, of her emotions, of her desires?

"Kiss me," he said.

She turned her face away from him, even though everything in her body was screaming that she should feast upon his lips. Even though she ached for his kisses, she resisted the impulse to indulge herself. It took all her willpower.

A moment later she felt his lips on her neck, just beneath her ear. As he kissed her neck, his deft hands skillfully caressed her breasts, moving and squeezing the exuberant mounds, using just the right amount of pressure when pinching her nipples to draw the absolute amount of pleasure without crossing into the territory of pain,

He's a master at seduction, she thought as she felt his tongue slide into her ear while his fingers tugged delightfully on her nipples through her dress and chemise. *He knows how to do everything precisely. Only a man with divine powers can possess such wisdom.*

She suspected she should hate him, or at least resent him at least a little . . . but she couldn't manage to summon up either emotion.

Caleb was speaking, saying words that she suspected she should pay careful attention to. They weren't polite words. They were lustful words coming from a man who did not put limits on his lustful ways.

I can't stop him, she thought. Her next thought was, *I don't want to stop him. Caleb can do with me whatever he wants . . . so long as he doesn't stop.*

For a woman who had lived, quite literally, for years worrying about what her powerful ex-husband would say about her in society, to think such a libidinous thought was an act of utter liberation. She sensed that Caleb was setting her soul free.

She felt his powerful hands raising her dress and chemise, lifting the hem high enough so that it was over her hips. The next barrier to her most precious place was her knickers. They were cotton, completely utilitarian, and not at all meant to be seen by a man who would appreciate them.

She wished that she'd worn prettier knickers . . . but she didn't own any pretty underclothing.

When Caleb didn't bother to unknot the drawstring, she

gasped. Instead, he pushed his fingers into the waistband at the small of her back and simply jerked the garment down to the middle of her thighs. He was not a man to let a woman's undergarments thwart his desires.

Chapter Two

Inga never realized she had always wanted a man like Caleb, but she'd never have met him unless a vicious divorce hadn't forced her to leave St. Louis and start a new life in Golden Valley, Montana. She decided she would try to feel lucky about that.

She tried to say something—it seemed as though she should voice some protest because that would be the ladylike thing to do—but words wouldn't form in her throat. In fact, she could hardly breathe.

She felt Caleb push the skirt of her dress, along with her simple cotton chemise, up to the small of her back. Her entire bottom was now exposed. She'd never felt quite so vulnerable, nor so desired.

"Fucking perfection," Caleb whispered.

She hadn't heard him use such a coarse curse word before. It shocked her now to hear it, and it pleased her that she was the one who had inspired it. She liked being able to inspire extremes in Caleb. With his experience in amour, she expected him to be more degage. It thrilled her that with her he wasn't cavalier.

She was distinctly aware of all the different sensations going through her body. The feel of the door against her face, against her breasts—it all gave her a sense of being trapped—and wantonly desired. An instant later, when Caleb cupped both of her buns in his wide-palmed hands and squeezed, she felt more naked than she'd ever felt in her life.

"Beautiful," she heard him say softly, his lips so close to her bottom that she could feel the heat of his breath. She felt his lips, warm and moist, kissing first one ass cheek and then the other. "Fucking beautiful," he said, then punctuated the comment by baring his teeth and lightly nipping at both of her ass cheeks.

His teeth hinted at pain, and a moment later his wet, tantalizing tongue glided over the skin he had just bitten and soothed away the discomfort. It was a combination of sensations that was unlike anything that Inga had ever before experienced. Nothing else could even come close to it. Because of it she uttered a sigh—it was actually more of a sob than a sigh—and she felt herself being sucked into an emotional whirlpool of sensations that she consciously knew she could not completely comprehend. She felt herself to be playing a game that had rules that she alone did not understand.

A little voice inside Inga's brain whispered that she should probably put an end to this lustful wickedness.

And then she felt him use his thumbs to pry apart her buns, and a moment after that, she felt his tongue caressing her taboo entrance.

Inga blasphemed again, but she forgave herself instantly for the transgression because she had never before felt anything that was so forbidden and so intense as Caleb's tongue on her bottom.

And then it got better. As he continued to tongue her backside, he slipped a thumb between the lips of her pussy, then used his forefinger to take control of her clit.

Caleb was tonguing her backside while using his thumb from inside her pussy and his finger from the outside to pinch and caress her clit. The combination of feelings was electrifying.

She'd kept her eyes squeezed tightly shut, but now they were wide open. So was her mouth. But she could not see anything, nor could she breathe. The feelings that Caleb's tongue, thumb, and fingertip were eliciting were more than she could lucidly comprehend.

"I'm going to come," she said softly, almost apologetically. Her Swedish accent was as thick as cold honey.

It seemed to her that she was responding more quickly, more enthusiastically, to what Caleb was doing to her than was either proper or ladylike.

That didn't make any difference just seconds later when a series of orgasmic spasms went through her that were countless times stronger than anything she'd ever before experienced. It was like ocean waves during the most violent of storms, one wave crashing against the shore, and then the next one following it immediately, and each one being as physically intense as the one before it.

After the sixth or seventh climactic convulsion went through her, she realized that she had at last reached the end of whatever sensual journey she was on. With her forehead pressed against the door and her hands near her face she whispered, "Please . . . you've got to stop. I can't take any more."

To her endless relief, Caleb did exactly what she asked of him.

She felt him release her bottom, and a moment later she sensed rather than felt as he rose to his feet. His presence seemed gigantic.

Now what happens to me? she wondered. The possibilities were as scary as they were enticing. She shivered at the thought of what might happen next.

Caleb kissed her on the temple, then the cheek. She thought of turning her face to kiss him—it seemed important since they had done some terribly intimate things together, and still they hadn't kissed—but she stopped herself. The time would come, she decided, when she would kiss him, but that time wasn't this time. Just not right now.

The here and now was all about savoring forbidden

delights. There wasn't anything about Caleb that wasn't forbidden and wasn't delightful.

He kissed the side of her mouth, and she turned her face away, but only slightly. She was denying him her mouth, but nothing else. He kissed the side of her neck, and the moan that Inga issued was an intentional invitation for him to do more of the same.

She felt his fingers curling around her hipbones, and for a moment hold her firmly. Then he took a half-step backward and pulled her with him. She found herself now with her arms straight out in front of her, palms against the wall. Her body was bent slightly at the waist. Her dress and chemise were still on the small of her back.

"Beautiful ass," Caleb muttered under his breath.

Oh, no, she thought, now on the edge of panic. *He's going to take me back there.*

But just when her fears were reaching their peak, she felt Caleb rubbing the plum-sized crown of his erection against the passion-swollen lips of her pussy, and she instantly was aware that what awaited her was ecstasy. Perhaps another time he'd take the back door, but not this time. She sensed, as a woman knew such things, that this wouldn't be the last time he'd have her.

She felt the pressure build as he tried to enter her body, and though she tried to relax to make the invasion easier, she could not. It didn't matter. Caleb was far too determined, and she was far too willing for there to not be penetration. She had no choice but to succumb, and she wouldn't have wanted it any other way.

She felt the lips of her pussy expanding, accommodating more manly flesh than had ever before been expected of her. Inga experienced a twinge of pain—it had been a long time since she'd been passionate—but the discomfort was nothing more than that, and a moment later, when she felt the long, thick shaft of Caleb's arousal pushing the plump crown deeper and deeper inside her, she felt the passion that she thought had been fulfilled begin to well up inside her feminine, passionate self once again.

Caleb could inspire a greedy libido. She accepted this as a fact. To argue otherwise was to deny reality.

Caleb was undoubtedly a lusty man, but he was a connoisseur of lovemaking, not a savage. He entered her slowly, by degrees, sliding deeper and deeper with each thrust but never using ramming force to get where he wanted to be. He understood that his size meant accommodation had to be made.

Thank you, Caleb, Inga thought. *It's been so long for me, and you're so big. If you were a brute this would be agony instead of ecstasy.*

When he thrust three-quarters of his length into her the next time, and then the full-length with his next thrust, his pelvis smacked against the cheeks of her ass as she trembled, standing while leaning against his office door. Inga thanked whatever gods that she believed in and even ones that she didn't believe in that Caleb was a connoisseur and not a savage. She felt herself to be profoundly fortunate that her lover was a gentleman and not a beast. His dimensions could be dangerous.

"So right," Caleb said quietly. The sound of his voice was distinctly erotic to her at that moment. "So . . . fucking . . . right. Precious. Nothing less than precious."

It was at that exact moment—when she heard what Caleb had said—that she felt the first indications that she was going to have another orgasm. And not only was she going to come again, but the next climax might be even more powerful than the previous one, and this was almost a scary thought since her entire body damned near turned inside out when Caleb tongued her backside while he pleasured her clit with a forefinger and thumb with skill that, as far as Inga could tell, only demigods and demons possessed.

Inga felt the long, smooth slide of Caleb's withdrawal, and

she told herself, *He's not a god. Maybe a demigod. But he's nothing less than that.*

No man has ever called me 'precious.' This thought came a moment before she whispered, "Don't stop."

Without hesitations, Caleb said, "Of course not, precious."

Inga hadn't expected the climax to hit her so quickly, or had she ever thought that it would hit her so violently. She started screaming and was aware that she was making too much noise, even though she knew that the one absolute thing she should never do under these circumstances was draw attention to herself.

From behind, Caleb put his palm over her mouth to silence her. Intellectually, rationally, her first emotion was to rebel at what he had done. A gentleman simply didn't put his hand over a woman's mouth while having sex.

It took only a second for her to realize that he was the rational one. He was the one who had not gone blind because of desire. There were people just outside the office door, and those people had ears. Her adoration of Caleb went up a notch. Actually, much more than that.

As the waves of pleasure subsided, while Caleb's hand remained firmly over her mouth and his hips continued their steady rhythm, she slowly descended from the heights of ecstasy that Caleb had brought her to.

She could tell by the sound of his ragged breathing, and by the increasing fury of his pistoning hips, that he was soon coming to a climax.

Tell him not to come inside me!

The thought screamed in her brain. It was vitally important that he not release his passion inside her. It could lead to the worst of all possible outcomes.

An instant later, Caleb plunged full-length, then withdrew completely.

"Uh!" was the sound that came from him through his nose, not his mouth. It was the only sound he made, and only she could hear it.

Inga felt the semen landing on her, hitting her from the back of her head to her buns. There were four thick streams—or were there five?—that erupted from him. She was consciously aware that Caleb's ejaculations were far more voluminous than her ex-husband's. This pleased her, though she couldn't say why.

She could feel semen, warm, thick, and creamy, trickling down from her bottom and moving slowly toward the insides of her thighs. She felt it in her hair, and she wasn't at all certain how she should feel about that.

He didn't come inside me, she thought with more gratitude than she'd ever had in her life. *He's not only gorgeous, he's responsible.*

"Inga," Caleb said softly, "are you alright?"

"I'm a mess . . ." she said after a moment. She touched the hair at the back of her head and felt sperm. She pushed herself away from the door and stood straight, smoothing her dress down over buttocks and thighs that had cooling semen dribbling down them. "But I'm fine. I'm grateful that you didn't ejaculate inside me, and I'm wondering how much Maggie heard. When you made me climax, I wasn't quiet about it."

"No," Caleb said, quirking an eyebrow over a chocolate brown eye glimmering with mischief and delight. "You weren't very quiet." He stepped forward and kissed her lightly on the forehead. "I'll make sure I have my hand over your mouth the next time I make you come."

In a soft voice that was both timid and anxious, she asked, "Will that be soon?"

"You can count on it."

His confidence, his masculine surety, nearly made her climax right then and there. There was nothing sexier to her than a self-confident man.

She didn't have an orgasm, but she knew she would soon. She was certain of it. Caleb inspired that kind of confidence.

CHAPTER THREE

Kimberly sat in the London-style hansom cab on Main Street of Golden Valley with her hands folded together in her lap. Nervously, she looked around at the morning crowd. On horseback or in carriages or hansom cabs, Golden Valley was a thriving, bustling, prosperous gold-rich city at this time of the morning. There was money to be made, and only a fool had idle hands.

For the third time since the hansom cab had come to a stop on the cobblestone street in front of the Cattleman's Emporium Saloon and Casino, she pulled out the small watch she kept in her purse. She opened the case with trepidation. It was almost eleven minutes past eight o'clock, which meant she was once again late to work—which was exactly as she had planned.

"That'll be all," she called out to the driver. Instantly, the twin front doors to her hansom cab were opened. "Thank you," she said as she got out. She handed the driver a coin.

The driver looked at what she'd given him, then grinned broadly, displaying the fact that he was missing several teeth on one side of his mouth. A fist can do that.

"Thank you, miss. Thank you very much. And if there's anything you need, you just come see me and I'll take you to it right quick."

Kimberly had tipped him handsomely because he hadn't complained when she had him stop outside the Cattleman's Emporium building and didn't insist she leave so that he could get another fare. He didn't even ask for more money.

She took one last look up and down Main Street, inhaled deeply of the clean Montana air several times to summon her courage, then walked into the building.

The dealers were at their tables. Even at this early hour there were men hoping this morning would be a lucky one for them at the gaming tables.

Without hurrying her stride—though she desperately wanted to—she walked to the stairs leading to the second floor of the building. A braided velvet rope was secured at the foot of the stairs, and a uniformed guard was standing on duty. When the two made eye contact, the guard immediately disconnected the rope so that Kimberly could make her way up to the executive floor, where all the really important decisions were made.

That was where she had her desk. Outside the spacious office shared by Adam Wright and Bryce Samuels, the men she worked for, and on this morning, had intentionally antagonized.

She stepped into the outer office. Maggie, the newest and by far the youngest of the office assistants, had a worried look on her face. Even before Kimberly could sit in her chair, Maggie whispered, "They said you're supposed to go see them the minute you arrive."

Kimberly felt her heart skip a beat. She set her purse on her desk and said under her breath, "Wish me luck. I think I'm going to need it. They hate it when I'm late."

She rapped lightly on the polished oak door with a plaque of silver with the names of Adam Wright and Bryce Samuels engraved on it. Immediately, a commanding voice called out, "Enter!"

That is not the voice of a happy man.

She turned the doorknob and stepped into the office. She kept her gaze down toward the floor so that she wouldn't look either of the men she worked for directly in the eyes.

Adam, the elder of the two executive vice presidents of the

Cattleman's Emporium business dynasty cleared his throat and then said in a low, ominous tone, "You're late once again, Kimberly. Do you remember what we said the last time you were late?"

She nodded and continued looking at the floor. She could feel her palms growing clammy and could feel her vagina getting moist with anticipation.

"We need an answer from you," Bryce said. "What did we tell you?"

"You said you would punish me if I was ever late again." There was a faint, tremulous quality to her voice that she was quite pleased with. She could feel her nipples tightening and become more sensitive. Between her legs, at the top of her sex, her clit was throbbing with anticipation.

She heard both men rise from their chairs. The click of their bootheels against the floor seemed as loud as a drum and as erotic as anything Kimberly had ever heard.

"I'm sorry I'm late," she lied. "I'm ready for my punishment," she said, this time telling the truth.

"Obviously, you need to be taught a lesson," Adam said.

She gasped softly, and for the first time since entering their private office, she looked up from the floor. When she looked at them, she couldn't decide which man was more handsome. And when she watched each unknotting and removing his black necktie, she knew she was in for an experience unlike anything she'd ever had in her life.

Adam moved so that he was directly in front of her, his ice-blue eyes glittering with a combination of menace and desire. As he looked straight into Kimberly's eyes, Bryce walked so that he was standing behind her.

Adam said, "You've brought this on yourself. You've only yourself to blame for what's about to happen."

Bryce said, "Put your hands behind your back. Put your wrists together."

She felt the lips of her pussy instantly swell slightly, responding to the command she had been given. When she put her wrists together, Bryce wound a silk necktie around her wrists twice, then tied the ends into a knot. At the sensation of being in bondage, Kimberly's knees began to tremble. She never looked anywhere but directly into Adam's eyes. She'd never felt so submissive, so under the command of dominating men . . . or so aroused.

Adam raised his necktie to about Kimberly's chin and said, "Now close your eyes."

When she did, he blindfolded her. Kimberly was now bound, blindfolded, with a heart that was racing in her chest and a pussy that was getting more creamy by the second.

"What . . . what are you going to do with me?" She could hardly get the words out she was so nervous.

She could hear the men begin walking around her, their boots unnaturally loud in an office that was silent as a tomb. Then she heard them moving chairs. She couldn't tell which boots belonged to which man. The mystery caressed her libido with a delicate touch.

She then felt them standing very close to her, but this time they were near her shoulders. Simultaneously, she had one large hand cupping one breast while another masculine hand cupped the other. She gaped softly. It was wickedly, wildly erotic for her to not know which man was which. The mystery added magic, and nothing was sexier than the unknown.

Do I dare say anything? It was a tempting question for her. Part of her wanted answers, but another part of her was wantonly thrilled with the mystery these men had put her in, her clit throbbing with tension.

Moving in unison, they began kneading and massaging her breasts through her chemise and the bodice of her dress. After a full thirty seconds of this, they began pinching and tugging on her nipples. Pleasure surged through her veins, and though she tried to remain absolutely silent, she couldn't keep a moan of desire to herself.

Kimberly found it difficult to keep her balance being blindfolded with her hands tied. She could feel that the hand on her right breast was pinching her nipple a bit more firmly than the one on the left, and she started wondering which man was the more forceful and which one the more gentle. The hands were equally erotic.

Once again two hands touched her simultaneously, this time below her waist. Again, Kimberly gasped. She had a hand caressing her sex through the front of her dress, and another squeezing the cheeks of her ass with enough force that she had no choice but to sexually respond. These were strong, confident hands that knew what they were doing, and knew it from experience.

It was the hand in front, the one that was in the most intimate way rubbing her rapidly heating vagina through her dress, chemise, and knickers that was the hand that galvanized her attention.

"Oh . . ." she sighed, her chin lowering to nearly touch her chest.

The hand between her legs, the one playing havoc with her sex and making the lubricating juices flow, was the one that focused her concentration. She was sensitive everywhere, but nowhere more than on her clit. All sensation seemed to emanate outward from there. It was the pulsing center of her universe.

I'll fall to the floor if they make me climax, she thought.

Summoning up willpower when she didn't think there was any, she promised herself that she wouldn't allow them to make her come. She decided, in a small act of defiance, that she wouldn't give them the satisfaction of making her climax.

This thought had just gone through her mind when she felt the men's palms slide downward very slowly, all the way down to her ankles. Then they started moving upward, but now they were beneath her dress, warm and strong hands raising first the hem, then chemise, sliding over her knickers, all the way up to her hips.

"Oh . . . oh . . ." she whispered.

Deft fingers unknotted the drawstring of her knickers with effortless ease. She felt the undergarment come loose around her hips. From each side of her body, fingers curled into her waistband and began pulling the cotton garment down past the curve of her hips.

She almost smiled then. For the planned occasion, she had chosen what she thought was her prettiest pair of knickers. They were snow-white and she'd worn them only once before. Around the bottom hem of the legs was a lovely strip of red embroidered lace that added a nice touch of color and femininity. They were meant to be seen as well as be functional.

A strong hand wrapped around her ankle and forcibly lifted her foot off the floor. After she'd eased her kidskin slippered foot out of the leg hole of her knickers, the process was repeated with the other foot.

She was surprised when the men let her dress and chemise fall back in place to cover her nudity.

She heard a wheeled office chair rolling closer, and the now-familiar sound of bootheels on the brightly polished slatwood floor. Strong hands grabbed her just above both elbows, squeezed tightly. She was moved by the men—she offered no resistance to their strength and determination—and then she felt herself bump into something with her knees and start to fall forward.

"Oh, no!" she said quickly, but in a whisper.

An instant later, Kimberly realized she was stretched over a man's lap as he sat in a chair. Her abdomen was against his thighs, her head angling downward toward the floor, her bottom now the uppermost part of her body. She felt more vulnerable than she'd ever been in her life.

The skirt of her dress and chemise were once again raised to the small of her back, but this time the pale mounds of her bottom were exposed. Kimberly could feel heat flow to her face and neck, and she knew she was blushing furiously.

Why don't they say something? They're torturing me by not letting me know who is doing what to me.

For a moment a warm, broad palm rested lightly on one cheek of her ass, the fingers kneading gently. Then the hand stopped touching her and Kimberly felt an instant pang of regret. The hand had given her pleasure, and she didn't want it to stop.

Smack!

The hand had come down swiftly, spanking her with enough force that she involuntarily tossed her head up and arched her back. Though her mouth opened, and she grimaced, she did not cry out, nor make so much as a single sound.

She got spanked a second, third, and fourth time. She was certain that by the last spank her pale buns were pink and with distinct handprints on them. Kimberly relaxed her body, slumping down over the lap she was on.

If she thought the punishment was over, she was wrong. She was soon being spanked by whoever was standing at her hip, and he was giving her every bit as much of a swatting as the first man. The strong, male hand spanked her cruelly, but now and then it caressed with a distinct gentleness. The dichotomy between pleasure and pain was profoundly erotic.

Her buns were stinging madly when the spanking finally ended. The men gave her a full minute to compose herself, letting her remain stretched out over a lap that had thighs which were thick with muscle. She shifted her body just a little as it was uncomfortable having so much of her weight pressing against her stomach against masculine thighs. It wasn't easy to breathe. It was then that she felt the formidable erection, separated by several layers of masculine and feminine clothing, pressing against her stomach.

Uh-oh, she thought. *Now I'm in trouble.*

But she knew she wasn't in *real* trouble. In the two months that she had seen working for Adam and Bryce, the looks that they'd given her had indicated a sensual interest, and they did it in the way she suspected an alpha lion looks at a lioness.

She was grabbed firmly above the elbows and bodily, physically hauled to a standing position. She wobbled a bit on her feet—the blindfold distorted everything—so the men continued to hold her by the arms until she steadied herself.

More bootheels against the hardwood floor. The men were circling her, making it completely impossible to guess which lap she had been stretched over. They had both spanked her. Of that she was certain. But there was much she didn't know . . . and the uncertainty was as erotic as anything she had ever experienced.

She felt the necktie blindfold being unknotted, and she wasn't certain if she was happy that the mystery was about to come to an end. She had discovered that there was a certain eroticism to the unknown.

She had to blink her eyes several times to clear her vision, but then she found herself standing in front of the gorgeous men she worked for. She'd never before seen such a devilish or enticing twinkle in two sets of eyes.

"Hello, Kimberly," Adam said, his gaze roaming with undisguised lust up and down over Kimberly's body. "It's nice that you could finally find the time to show up for work."

Before she could say anything, Bryce raised his hand, and the look in his eyes warned her that she would hold her tongue or she could expect to suffer the consequences—and she knew what that could mean.

"Before you lie to me with those luscious lips, there's

something I want to do first," Adam said, his voice a low growl.

"What's that?" she asked. She couldn't help herself. The instant the words were out of her mouth, she wished she'd said nothing at all.

"Kiss them."

Chapter Four

Kimberly drew a ragged breath and held it. The intensity she saw in Adam's eyes should have frightened her, but it didn't. She had planned to incite a powerful response, and that's exactly what she was getting. She never expected both of them to come at her though. And she certainly never anticipated the neckties. It seemed to her now that there were so many things that she hadn't planned on—just as she didn't anticipate her own vagina's clenching response to the bondage and spanking. It was instantaneous, shockingly receptive, and unquestionably a taboo pleasure . . . and those, Kimberly was discovering, were the best kind.

A shiver coursed through her when the men approached her. Adam was slightly to her right, and Bryce slightly to her left. It was Adam who reached out with both hands and placed them on her face. He held her firmly as he began lowering his face slowly toward hers. Kimberly closed her eyes. A moment later she felt his mouth seal over hers. His lips were warm, and though they were soft, the kiss was commanding.

She felt Adam's tongue touch her lips. She parted them, and his tongue eased into her mouth and began dancing with hers.

As she kissed Adam, Bryce began fondling her breasts through her dress and chemise. She was full-bosomed and when her nipples became erect, their aroused condition was visible even through several layers of clothing.

The soft moan that drifted to her ears came from herself.

Adam turned her head to the side, ending the kiss, but not his mouth's busy pleasure-giving. He sucked on her earlobe for a moment, then began kissing her taut throat. Occasionally he bared his teeth and nipped at her sensitive skin. She gasped when Adam soothed the discomfort he had caused by licking it away.

In a soft, tremulous voice, she whispered with a certain helplessness, "I don't know what to do."

"We're in control now," Bryce said in a low growl. And then, as though to prove his point, he caught both of her erect nipples through her clothing and gave them a firm pinch and twist.

She tossed her head back and gasped more loudly than she suspected she should. It was impossible to remain completely silent even though she was vividly aware that Maggie was at her desk in the inner office so nearby.

As Adam kissed his way back up to her mouth, he put his hand on her bottom. A moment later, he began pulling her dress up her legs from in front and in back. She had the suspicion that she should stop him, but she did not.

"I've been aching to kiss you," Adam said, his lips brushing erotically against hers as he spoke, "since the first moment you walked into this office."

From the first moment!

The words were like a narcotic to her rapidly escalating desire. She suddenly felt disoriented with a passion she could not control. When Adam kissed her mouth again, she opened her lips invitingly, and the kiss they shared was the deepest and most intimate one yet. When the kiss ended, she could only wonder what would happen next.

Bryce began unbuttoning her dress, starting at her throat and working his way swiftly and expertly down to her waist. Once that was accomplished, he started on the four small, cloth covered buttons of her chemise that ran from her bodice to her navel.

Two things happened precisely at the same time. Adam's right hand pushed up between her naked thighs to touch the moist lips of her pussy, and Bryce's mouth captured the crest of her left breast. One sensation magnified the other, and combined, they were electrifying.

"Ohhh," she sighed as a myriad of feelings bombarded her senses.

She'd never before felt so much stimulation at one time in so many different places on her body. The pads of Adam's middle two fingers began caressing her clit with a circular motion, using just the right amount of pressure to elicit the greatest degree of pleasure. As this was happening, Adam turned his attention to her other breast. When he sucked all of her nipple and much of her areola into his mouth, the ecstasy was so intense it was almost painful. Almost. But not quite. And that made all the difference in the universe.

She could feel the orgasm begin to form within herself, starting at some nebulous place somewhere between her hipbones. The climax was starting slowly, but she could feel it approaching. She could feel it distinctly. It was like a thunderstorm on the Dakota plains where a person can see for many miles and watch the dark, ominous clouds rolling closer and closer.

She sensed that the storm would bring with it thunder, lightning, and torrential rain. It would be an event so intense it would bring with it destruction and carnage, and the thought of what she would be like when the storm had passed caused her to moan into Adam's mouth as he sucked on her tongue.

Bryce opened her chemise wider and kissed the lower slope of her breast, then her stomach.

"Hold her," Bryce said, then bit her lightly on the stomach. She flinched. "Hold her tight."

Adam took his hand from between her legs, bunched the

front of her dress in his fist and moved slightly to the side as Bryce got down on his knees on the office's hardwood floor. The two moved as though their actions were choreographed. Their moves weren't rehearsed, but it seemed as though they were.

She sucked in her breath and held it as Bryce, with her dress held high, looked at her pussy for long seconds, then tilted his head back and looked up into her eyes.

"I'll bet you taste as fresh as raindrops."

The words were very nearly enough to make her climax. It was almost impossible for her to fathom the fact that she had her hands bound behind her back, and one of the most handsome men she'd ever met in her life was on his knees in front of her. She watched as he kissed the inside of her leg, high on her thigh. When he tapped the inside of her legs, she spread her feet a little wider apart and now it was impossible to breathe regularly. Either she was gulping in air at a furious pace, or she was holding her breath. For a moment she wondered if her heart was beating so strongly that Maggie could hear her through the walls.

She was most assuredly in a hurry to have the next phase of this encounter begin, but Bryce was apparently quite willing to be leisurely and savor the moment because he was taking his time kissing the naked, quivering inside of one thigh, and then the other. She was distinctly aware that his lips were warm and wet . . . and exquisitely skilled.

Looking down between the quivering mounds of her breasts, she watched as Bryce brought his face very close to her pussy, then he inhaled deeply through his nostrils. He sighed afterward as though he had just sniffed the cork of a vintage bottle of wine. She felt honored.

Her mouth opened wide, but she remained silent when Bryce brought his mouth to the lips of her pussy then leisurely began licking up and down between her petals. His movements were slow and sensual and meant to please her to the marrow of her bones.

"Oh, God! Oh, God!" she whispered, her eyes open wide as she watched what was being done to her. The voyeur in her blossomed.

It was spectacular when Bryce licked the lips of her pussy, but when he captured her clit between his lips while at the same time easing his middle finger into her, the fire within her became an inferno in an instant. The lusty conflagration was immediate. These men, she realized, had turned up the heat in a big way.

She felt Adam moving at her side, but she couldn't pay him much attention. Not when Bryce was using his lips, tongue, and fingers with such devastating skill. But still, a small passion-fogged corner of her brain wondered what was about to happen next.

"I was right," Bryce said, his lips brushing her clit as he spoke. "You do taste like a raindrop."

Her knees nearly buckled when she heard the words. No man had ever said anything like that to her before.

Who wouldn't want to taste like a raindrop?

Adam had moved to stand directly behind her. She was looking down, watching Bryce pleasuring her sex with an expertise that she had never before experienced. In fact, he was so good at delighting her with his mouth and fingers that she wasn't even aware, at first, that she had curled the fingers of her right hand around the pulsing shaft of a very thick, solid-as-rock cock.

Once she realized what she had in her hand, she gave it a firm squeeze. When she did, Adam bent down and uttered a low groan of pleasure directly into her ear. He pulled back, then pushed forward again. She trembled as his cock slid through her fist before the crown of his erection rubbed against her just above the cleavage of her buns.

He's big. Very big.

The awareness brought with it equal measures of anticipation and anxiousness. She had some experience with men, but not a great deal of it. But she certainly had no experience with a man of Adam's size. He set a new standard, but she wasn't certain she wanted the bar to be set that high or there might be consequences she hadn't counted on.

That thought made her shiver from head to toe. Of the four lovers she'd had in her life, one had wanted to take her *back there.* Since she was in love at the time—or at least *thought* she was in love—she reluctantly agreed to give it a try. But her lover was more enthusiastic than he was skillful, and the sensual experiment was quickly abandoned when he used force instead of finesse.

It was one of the most utterly miserable sexual experiences she had ever experienced in her life.

She didn't know, at the time, that she would have more miserable experiences. There were many things she didn't know back then.

Her disturbing thoughts were quickly forgotten when she felt Bryce using his lips on her clit as he slipped his first two fingers deep inside her. She realized that the climax which seemed so far off in the distance was now rushing headlong toward her and much closer that she had expected. She could almost hear the coal-fired steam engine charging at full-speed.

Adam was pumping his hips a bit faster now, and with more determination. The head of his cock struck her in the back, then slid upward each time he pushed at her.

Every sensation she experienced was entirely new to her even though at twenty-eight she certainly was not a virgin. She was in such a frenzied emotional state that she was willing to do anything—anything at all—that Adam and Bryce told her she must do. Even if it meant taking Adam's thick cock between the cheeks of her ass.

But that was a scary thought. She'd already done that with another man, and it hadn't felt good. In fact, it hurt a lot. And he wasn't nearly the man that Bryce was.

Adam and Bryce had aroused her so thoroughly that she was incapable of denying them anything, no matter what they demanded of her. In the oddest of all possible ways, she simultaneously felt utterly helpless against their desires and all-powerful because of the lust she had inspired in them. They brought out in her emotions that were polar opposites.

"Oh, no," she whispered.

She started to bend forward at the waist, but Adam whipped an arm over her shoulder, his hand coming down directly over her firm breast. He hauled her upright instantly.

Adam pinched her nipple as Bryce sucked and fingered her pussy. And that's when the contractions began. Harsh, convulsive spasms that made her want to bend over, but Adam had too powerful of a hold on her for that to happen. Wave after wave of desire shuddered through her as she climaxed on Bryce's mouth. As she came, Bryce continued his glorious assault on her senses by continuing to suck on her clit, no matter how strenuously she shook her hips.

When the climax was finally over, her legs could no longer hold her weight. Adam and Bryce kept her standing for several seconds as she gulped in air and blinked her eyes, trying to clear her vision.

"Let her down," Bryce said quietly as he got to his feet in front of her. "It's time for her to get on her knees and stay there until we say otherwise."

They eased her down until she was kneeling in the center of the office, her dress unbuttoned to her waist and her chemise open. Her breasts were exposed, and her nipples were still moist from the mouth that had feasted so ravenously on them. She was still breathing deeply in post-orgasmic bliss with her head down and her eyes closed when the men positioned themselves at her shoulders.

She felt Adam pull the two ivory combs that kept her hair in a tight bun at the base of her neck. Her long, raven black hair fell down her back, still twisted round into a silken rope. Adam bent and fluffed her hair, easing his fingers into the strands so that instead of being twisted round and round, her hair now fell loose and straight down her back.

When he'd accomplished his task, he stroked her hair several times from the crown of her head down to the back of her neck.

"So beautiful," he whispered sincerely. His voice touched her in ways that even his fingers couldn't.

The simple sentence delighted her. When she tested the necktie surrounding her wrists, she found—as she knew she would—that she was securely bound, and that her wrists would not be freed until these men decided she should be. She tested the necktie again, and, confident that she was securely bound, felt her pussy clench and become just a little moister, a bit more sensitive and ready for stimulation.

Adam's fingers combed into her hair at the crown of her head, his fingertips burying enough to graze against her scalp. Then his hand tightened into a fist, and she felt strands of her hair pulling against her scalp. She winced but said nothing as Adam tilted her head back on her shoulders so that he could look into her eyes.

"So beautiful," he said, his eyes glittering with a desire that was almost feral. He held her hair with his left hand while his right was holding an erection of formidable dimensions. He held it like other men might hold a weapon. "An enchantress who may open the gates of hell."

He brought the head of his cock to her mouth. She didn't resist. She kissed the knob. When it pushed against her lips, she opened them. He eased in softly, smoothly, forcing her jaws to open wider and wider. She sheathed her teeth with her lips. This certainly wasn't the first time that she'd had an erection in her mouth, but it was the first time that, while holding just the crown in her mouth, she could hardly fit any more of the manly flesh inside. Adam was much more man than she'd previously had to deal with.

While holding her securely by the hair, Adam withdrew until only the very tip of his cock was between her lips. She used her tongue against the slit in the tip before Adam pushed forward again, this time not stopping until his crown was pressing firmly against the opening of her throat. Her tongue was pressed flat when she held him in her mouth. She hadn't known a man could be such a mouthful.

She began to squirm on her knees when Adam continued to press his bulbous cockhead against the back of her mouth. The pressure against her throat was constant. She began to worry that he would choke her with his rigid flesh. Then, just when she was certain that she was about to gag, Adam withdrew, and she was once again able to breathe comfortably.

How do they always know how to push the limit without going too far?

Adam pumped his hips, driving his cock several more times between her lips and deep into her mouth, then he released the grip he had on her hair, setting her free.

"I was wondering when you'd get around to sharing," Bryce said, an edge to his tone. "You can have a selfish streak in you every once in a while." He looked down at Kimberly. "She inspires selfishness—especially when she's on her knees."

She did not protest when Bryce combed his fingers into her hair, tightened his hand into a fist, then turned her head in his direction.

"Suck," Bryce indelicately commanded as he pushed his cockhead first against her lips, then between them.

After that, with her eyes closed, she turned her head left and right while remaining on her knees, first sucking one cock, then the other, giving pleasure with her mouth with more enthusiasm than she had ever before in her life. The commanding, dominating nature of the men she was with made surrendering to them, being submissive to them, seem not only natural, but exquisitely erotic. There wasn't a nerve in her body that wasn't vibrantly alive.

Will they want more than just my mouth?

CHAPTER FIVE

Kimberly shocked herself when she realized that she hoped they wanted all of her. Well, perhaps not *all,* but certainly most, and more than just her mouth. She felt her bottom clench. She didn't know if her body was responding to fear or anticipation.

"Get her up," Adam said as he grabbed her by the upper arm. Bryce did the same, and together they lifted her to her feet. "To my desk."

They marched her the short distance to his desk. Indelicately, they pushed her so that she was bent over the solid mahogany surface, her naked breasts becoming even more round as they compressed against the desktop. The awareness of being in bondage heightened every sensation she experienced. She felt she was on the brink of bursting into flames.

She'd never felt so vulnerable nor so alive.

She felt her dress and chemise once again being lifted to the small of her back. It was Adam who was behind her. She was about to get what she so desperately wanted from him even though she could never verbally admit to needing. He seemed to *know* what she wanted without having to be *told* what she wanted. It was just one of the many things she adored about him.

"Gorgeous," Adam said, rubbing the crown of his erection up and down over the honeyed lips of Kimberly's entrance. "Unbelievable."

She tried to relax. She turned her face to the side, then let her cheek press against the desktop as she waited for the sensation of having her body invaded by Adam. There was a wicked eroticism in having her wrists bound behind her back while another virile man was there, watching everything, waiting for his turn to ravish her.

She was aware that this encounter was far from over. She shivered at the thought of what the next hours held in store for her.

For the first time in her life, she wondered just how many orgasms she would have. She took great pleasure in pondering the question.

She was a little surprised at Adam. She had expected him to be brutish, but he most certainly wasn't. He entered her slowly, only a little of his magnificent length invading her tight channel before retreating. Her body had never had to expand as much as it needed to for her to accommodate Adam, but to her fathomless relief, all she felt was an overwhelming sense of fullness without the slightest bit of pain. The man was very thick, but he knew how to control himself. She thought, *Thank you.*

It was on the eighth revolution of his hips that she felt Adam's pelvis against the cheeks of her ass. She had taken every throbbing inch of his erection into her body and all she felt was an incredible sense of completion.

You don't have to be so gentle.

The thought came to her, and it surprised her when she was aware of it. She almost said the words aloud, but then thought better of it. Telling a man like Adam that he didn't have to be such a gentleman with her might get her more of a response than she wanted. But wasn't that what she really wanted? This was a question that tantalized her libido. The one thing she was aware of was that she didn't know the answer. She wasn't even certain she wanted the answer.

Adam's hips were like a piston in a steam engine. They started out moving slowly, but with each revolution, they moved faster and faster. She heard the sound of Adam's pelvis colliding with her buns as his cock plowed deep into her. She gasped each time he reached full insertion, the breath being forced from her lungs as she was driven into the desk. She felt the sharp edge of the desktop at the exact juncture of where her leg and torso met, and in a distant corner of her brain, she wondered whether she would have bruises because of it.

Smack!

She tossed her head up, her eyes opening wide. She had thought that the spanking was over, but apparently she was wrong. The sensation of having a long, thick cock pumping into her while she was being simultaneously spanked was dizzyingly erotic.

Smack! Smack! Smack!

Her buns were stinging now, and she was quite certain they were pink from the abuse Adam had given them. She'd never experienced anything so erotic. It touched her in places that had never before experienced sensual pleasure.

Smack!

This time the spank had brought with it her awareness that yet another climax was approaching, but this time it wasn't a long way off, it was practically upon her when she first became aware of it. She could hear the roar of the engines. This time she wasn't going to climax, she was going to explode.

Then she felt Adam grab her by the hips with both hands. His fingers bore into her flesh. His labored breathing sounded like the engine of a train that was running at full speed. Time and time again she was pounded against the side of the desk. She felt she was being ravaged, and it was exquisite in the extreme.

"I'm going to—" she said, but then the intensity of the moment became too powerful for her to speak. A sound came out of her throat as though she was choking.

Her vagina clenched and relaxed and then clenched again

around Adam's pounding cock as the climax claimed her. She clenched her teeth, but she didn't cry out as pulsing, white hot desire gripped her. Her lips pulled back in a grimace of wanton satisfaction. She didn't make a sound, but her mind was screaming.

She was still shivering through her orgasm when Adam withdrew completely. He groaned, and she felt his sperm, thick and sticky, splashing against her buns. As she felt his passion dribbling down the insides of her thighs, she breathed a sigh of relief that he'd shown the sensual discipline to not release his sperm inside her.

Her estimation of the kind of man that Adam was had just gone up astronomically. He'd just *not* committed her one unforgivable sin. Even in the throes of her emotional climactic turmoil, she wondered how she would repay him for his thoughtfulness.

"Give her a minute," Adam said, breathing deeply as he backed away from Kimberly, who remained bent over his desk. "Then it's your turn."

I'm not done. There's still one more stallion I've got to satisfy.

She waited, somewhat impatiently, for what would happen next. She knew this morning's erotic activities wouldn't be finished until she had sexually satisfied both of the men she worked for. These weren't the type of men who went unfulfilled. Ever.

"A minute's up," Bryce said.

The timbre of his voice made her shiver. There seemed to be something threatening in it. Or was it just steely determination? She couldn't tell, but a moment later, when he had slipped his fingers into her dress at the back of her neckline then unceremoniously pulled her to a standing position, she realized that what she'd heard in his voice was red-hot lust only barely kept in check by whatever civility he still possessed.

Bryce escorted her to the sofa with all the delicacy he used when he escorted his latest hooligan out of the saloon. He turned her around and planted an almost bruising kiss on her lips, then gave her a push. She tumbled backward onto the long, leather sofa.

Bryce's trousers were at the tops of his thighs, and his arousal was long and pale and visibly throbbing. It was also at face-level to Kimberly as she sat on the sofa with her hands still bound behind her back.

She leaned forward, her body language speaking as clearly as if she'd said the words aloud.

Bryce eased his hand around the back of her neck. He whispered, "My sweet . . ."

He brought the knob of his erection to her mouth. Kimberly opened her lips in invitation. A moment later her cheeks were hollowed as she drew a strong suction on the masculine flesh. Her eyes closed slowly, as someone might when falling asleep. For her, it was because she was entering an emotional place where nothing existed but what she felt, and what sublime emotions these men were capable of inspiring in her. She made a sound in her throat very much like a kitten purring. With Bryce's cock in her mouth, she salivated. She'd been on her knees before, but this was the first time her mouth watered because of it.

Bryce moved his hips slowly, easing his rigid manhood back and forth between her lips. Though she suspected that he was currently behaving about as civilized as he was capable of under the circumstances, she also suspected that the clock was ticking on his discipline.

He was a gentleman now, but he might well turn into a barbarian in just seconds. She'd had enough experience with men to know they could become someone else entirely in an instant.

"No more," Bryce said softly. She could hear the lusty tension in his voice. "Lay back. I can't take much more of you without exploding."

With a firm but not violent push, Bryce sent her tumbling backward so that her head and shoulders were against the backrest of the sofa, and her bottom was at the very edge of the seat cushions. He was on the floor between her spread knees a moment later.

"I can't wait much longer," he said, cock in hand, rubbing his crown against the slick lips of her vagina.

She whispered, softly but honestly, "You don't have to wait. Not on my account. I'm so ready."

She kept her eyes open, looking at the varying expressions on Bryce's face as he pushed himself into her. When he was fully embedded in her, he tilted his head back and gave a soft sigh that touched her to the core of her soul.

The feeling of being of being coddled didn't last long. She was on the sofa with her head and shoulders against the back cushion and her knees were spread wide . . . when Bryce went from a canter to a gallop. He grabbed her breasts and squeezed them firmly though briefly before he gripped her hips. His torso began powering his iron-hard cock in and out of her with such speed and force that she gasped each time his pelvis hammered against hers.

She felt her breasts, unencumbered without the constraints of either her chemise or the bodice of her dress, roll back and forth, moving with the jolting collision of Bryce's thrashing masculine body against her own feminine one. She gasped each time he reached full insertion, his sweaty body smacking against her own.

He's going to kill me with his cock. He's going to fuck me to death.

This thought would have frightened her, but hardly had the thought gone through her mind when yet another climax claimed her, this one hitting her without so much as a split-second of warning. As her body convulsed and contracted around Bryce's seesaw thrusts, she twisted and squirmed on the sofa, her movements hampered because her hands were still tied behind her body.

Even in the throes of orgasmic ecstasy, Kimberly understood that the necktie around her wrists was just one of the ingredients that was making this erotic meal so scrumptious. It added the element of taboo, and though she was new to passion, which was forbidden, she understood with an instinctual certainty that these were the men destiny had decided she should be with, and that they would teach her more truths about herself than she could ever possibly learn on her own.

They were her guides on this journey of self-discovery.

"Awww," Bryce growled as he withdrew from her silken vaginal embrace for the last time.

She watched as a thick, milky white stream of cream spewed from the head of Bryce's cock. The river was headed straight at her face. She closed her eyes and turned her face sharply to the side. A moment later she felt the come, warm and gooey, hit her on the temple very near her ear. She now had a line of cream from her cheek to her navel. Several more eruptions followed. Though she had always insisted on coitus interruptus with her lovers, she'd never before known a man who, in a single orgasm, could produce so much sperm.

Narcissistically, she wanted to believe that she was singularly responsible for such excess. In the back of her mind, she felt victorious . . . though she didn't exactly understand precisely why she should feel that way.

Seconds passed. Finally, Bryce rose to his feet. He was breathing deeply, and as she looked up at him, she could tell that he was completely and thoroughly pleased, and that she was the cause of his satisfaction. Even more importantly, the expression in his eyes was nothing less than limitless adoration.

Very softly, unsure of what was expected of her, she said,

"Can . . . can I get cleaned up? You can tie me up again whenever you want to, but you've made quite a mess of me, and I really must get washed up and back to my desk quickly or rumors are going to start." She sat upright on the sofa. "You'll do this to me again, won't you? With the neckties?"

Maggie could feel the tension in the office, and it worried her. Both Inga and Kimberly seemed ill-at-ease. They had gone into the private offices of the men they worked for, and both had stayed in those offices longer than they usually did. When they emerged to return to their desks and their duties, there wasn't the usual light banter that the three of them shared, and neither woman seemed willing to make direct eye contact with her. When they wouldn't look her in the eyes was when Maggie started getting nervous. In Maggie's world, eye contact was critical.

Were the men angry about something? She could understand if Adam and Bryce had given Kimberly a tongue-lashing. She had been late for work, after all, and she'd already been warned that such behavior wouldn't be tolerated. But Kimberly's coiffure wasn't quite as neat and tidy as it had been when she'd first stepped into the office, and Maggie couldn't help but wonder if they'd given her something more strenuous than just a cussing-out verbal warning. Did they rough her up? While Adam and Bryce were certainly powerful and domineering men, it didn't seem to Maggie that they were the kind of men who would use physical violence against a woman.

But still, Kimberly's hair had obviously been mussed up, and then she'd had to redo her coiffure as best she could. That much couldn't be ignored, though Maggie wasn't sure exactly what such paltry evidence meant. She was trying hard to not think the worst.

She looked over at Inga. The woman was studiously reading some of the telegraph messages that had come in with the latest batch. She seemed to be reading each message two or three times, as though she couldn't remember what she had just read. This troubled Maggie since Inga was one of the brightest women she'd ever met. And she was an absolute stickler for detail.

Something is troubling her. She can't concentrate on what she's reading.

Maggie crossed her fingers and hoped that whatever was wrong would soon be right.

Chapter Six

It had been weeks of bliss, and Inga was feeling a kind of contentment that she'd never known in her life. Since she and Caleb had taken the *next step* in their relationship and had become intimate, her sex life was multi-orgasmic, her love life was bliss, and her work life was just exactly as it had been prior to falling to the seductive charms of Caleb Essex. Except now she *really* looked forward to working at the Cattleman's Emporium Saloon and Casino.

She was, as the saying goes, walking on clouds every single day, from the time she woke up in her hotel room bed, to the time she returned to it.

Being near Caleb made her constantly feel as though ecstasy was just a heartbeat away.

The only thing that was missing was that she wasn't spending nights with Caleb, though he had assured her he would put an end to that problem somehow. The issue—as was so often the case in Golden Valley—was that there were gossips aplenty, and even though Golden Valley was a nearly lawless goldrush town with money in pockets and plenty of double-barreled shotguns with sawn barrels to make them more deadly at short range, there was still an elite upper-crust that insisted decorum must be maintained. And Caleb was a second-generation card-carrying member of Montana's most elite society.

The clock on the wall chimed. It was five o'clock. Inga felt a flutter in her heart, and she glanced guiltily over at Maggie. Five o'clock meant Inga was expected to go into Caleb's private office to see if he had any final assignments for her to fulfill.

At least that was the official line. Or was it the official lie?

Five o'clock is when he likes to get frisky.

She kept the smile she felt in her heart from showing on her face. She liked it when Caleb wanted to *fool around.* Sometimes he liked to make love, and sometimes he was satisfied with foreplay and teasing and lighthearted banter. But at other times he wanted more than that, and when he did, she never denied whatever he wanted from her. Sometimes he put her on her hands and knees in front of his desk and hammered into her from behind. At other times she was on her back, kissing him passionately as he pounded her into the leather-covered sofa. Sometimes she was fully dressed and, on her knees, pleasuring him to satisfaction with her mouth. Sometimes he was the one on his knees, pleasuring her to orgasmic bliss with his hands and tongue and his too-erotic-for-words lips.

When he sucked on her clit, she was completely incapable of anything even close to resembling coherent thought. She couldn't even speak with any credible clarity.

This awareness didn't disturb her in the least. Trading ecstasy for rational thought seemed a very small price to pay for that which was beyond measurable value.

"I'll go see to Caleb," she said to Maggie. "It's five."

"Should I come along?" Maggie said quickly. "I could help you."

"Not this time," Inga replied.

Maggie had made it clear several times that she wanted to learn everything there was to make Caleb happy. Whenever she said that Inga always wanted to smile, she kept the smile to herself. If Maggie *really* wanted to please Caleb, it would mean she'd have to do so much more for him than simply take dictation, getting the telegrams and newspapers from the telegraph office near the railroad station, and making sure that he had responded to all correspondence that he felt were important enough for him to pay attention to.

"But sometime soon?" Maggie asked. In her eyes was hopeful anticipation.

Inga looked at the girl. She was young—just eighteen, which made her exactly twenty years younger than Inga—and quite beautiful. Sometimes Inga wondered why Caleb had chosen to turn his romantic and lusty attention to her instead of the girl. After all, what powerful businessman didn't want a *young*, attractive, and adoring mistress to entertain himself with? Caleb was a man who had his choice of sexual partners.

Thirty-eight was no wealthy man's idea of a young woman. Yet Caleb had chosen her instead of Maggie. Why? The question haunted her, mostly when she was trying to get to sleep at night. She tried hard to not think about it, but she couldn't help herself because she was not young, and Maggie most certainly was.

"Yes," she said after a few moments of deliberation. She could see the hunger for acceptance in the girl's expression. "I promise. Sometime soon."

Maggie's smile was open and honest, and in her blue eyes was a combination of relief and excitement that Inga found utterly, thoroughly charming.

She grabbed her notebook and the two pencils she'd sharpened that morning, then got out of her chair and walked the short distance to Caleb's office door. She had to remind herself that she mustn't run, and she should appear to be not wanting to see Caleb as much as she really did.

On some days, when it got to be three o'clock or so, she could hardly keep from staring at the large clock on the wall, wishing that the seconds would pass more quickly so that it would be five o'clock and she would have a legitimate excuse to go into Caleb's office and close the door behind herself.

Relax. He's probably too busy with work. He won't have time to fool around. It's probably best that way.

Inga knocked softly on the door and immediately heard Caleb call out, "Come in."

When she opened the door, she found Caleb hunched over his desk, his gold pen in hand. He appeared to be making changes to a contract, and his concentration was focused. He made no outward indication that he was aware that he was no longer alone. She read his body posture instantly and accurately.

She closed the door very carefully, making almost no sound at all. She walked closer to his desk, stepping on the Persian rug that was twelve feet long and six feet wide, and oval shaped. Adam and Bryce had ordered one for their shared office, and when Caleb saw it, he'd ordered an identical rug for his own office.

She walked up to the desk, but she said nothing. She could see the contract that Caleb was editing. It was an important one—she remembered it dealt with railroad transportation of lumber from northwestern Canada south to the rapidly expanding city of San Francisco. There was, as Caleb had explained to her, money to be made in helping a city grow. A fortune, actually.

"Gold is a wonderful commodity," Caleb had told her just the other day. "But without lumber, city expansion comes to a screeching halt. It is as simple as that. Civilization needs cut lumber to flourish, to expand and grow. America needs lumber like a new-born baby needs mother's milk."

Caleb had been in negotiations with a Canadian firm when he'd said that to her. Inga, whose penmanship was flawless, was the one he had assigned to write the contract in longhand.

She watched him put a line of ink through three entire lines of the contact, then set his gold pen down horizontally on the holder on his desk, inhaled deeply before exhaling, then he pushed his chair away from his desk.

After several seconds he looked up at her. When their

gazes met, he smiled broadly. The expression in his eyes said he couldn't be happier than to have her in his office with him.

His happiness shouldn't mean so much to me . . . but it does.

"I thought I'd come in and see if you have any last-minute assignments for me."

Inga found it very difficult to not smile. The seriousness Caleb had displayed when he was editing the contract vanished completely, replaced with a buoyancy of spirit that she always found unabashedly delightful. There was nothing about the man that didn't delight her.

"Have a seat," Caleb said with mock seriousness. "I'm sure I can think of something for you to do."

There were no chairs. That fact rather significantly limited her seating options.

She walked around his desk. Caleb was sitting on his chair with his knees spread wide apart. She stepped between his legs, then sat on his right thigh and placed her notebook and the two pencils on his desk. Some days she opened her notebook and held her pencil poised at the ready . . . and some days, when she sat on his leg, she knew from the look in his eyes that she was going to be doing a lot more than just taking dictation.

"How has your day been?" Caleb asked with deceptive casualness as, with his left hand, he began slowly pulling her dress up her legs. "Did you finish the tasks I gave you this morning?" His fingers grazed lightly up the inside of her calf.

"Yes, s—"

She was able to stop herself from completing the sentence. She'd almost said sir, because something that was part of a little game she played with Caleb. The rules, she was learning, could shift day by day.

His hand was now on her knee beneath her dress, inching slightly higher so that his fingertips were caressing her inner thigh in a slow, leisurely circular motion. She was pretending not to notice what he was doing to her, but she was intensely aware of his touch, and how it fired up the lusty desires that were always percolating within her whenever she was in the same room with him.

"How is Maggie working out for you?" Caleb asked, his caresses moving toward the middle of her tapering, naked thigh. She could feel the tingling in her clit. "Is she proving to be helpful? Is she causing you any problems?"

She spread her knees just a little wider apart. It was a silent invitation. She knew where Caleb's magnificently talented hand was going, and she didn't want anything to slow, and certainly not stop its journey. She resisted the urge to kiss him. Sometimes he liked to play a game where he touched her intimately while she pretended nothing illicit was happening.

It was a game she liked a lot, especially when she stopped pretending and Caleb got down on his knees, magnificently handsome and fully dressed in hand-tailored clothes . . . and gave her oral sex until she thought her skin was going to start on fire, and the top of her head was going to blow right off.

"No problems," she said. "She wants me to teach her how to please you. She's very naïve to ask such a question."

"Or maybe she's just curious. She had a pretty rough introduction to the ways of romance back home in Helena."

"You know about that?"

Inga was surprised that Caleb knew, but only a little He was a man who seemed to know everyone's secrets. In fact, he seemed to make it his business to know everyone else's secrets.

"Not the details. She's the daughter of a friend of a good friend and business associate of mine. Apparently, she got messed up with the wrong young man and her reputation got besmirched beyond repair. She had to get out of town and that's how she ended up in my office."

"I've sort of become her big sister, it seems. She confides in me. What happened was that she got involved with a rich man's son who promised her the moon, but that wasn't enough for her to lose her virtue over. He begged and pleaded, and she finally relented to his wishes, but with conditions."

"Conditions?" Caleb's right eyebrow lifted in haughty inquiry. He stopped caressing the inside of her thigh, concentrating now on her words.

"She agreed, but on the condition that he never tell anyone what they'd done, and that he not climaxes inside her."

"Smart girl. Doesn't sound naïve to me. Sounds damned intelligent."

"Well, she sure as hell put her trust in the wrong man. She told me they did you-know-what three nights in a row. On all three nights he climaxed inside her. Then he bragged to anyone who'd listen about how often they were doing it. He was also having sex with a shopkeeper's daughter, and she wasn't quite so concerned about not getting pregnant, since the boy's family is worth a fortune, and she wants a slice of it. When Maggie said she couldn't—or at least wouldn't—have sex with him anymore, he told even more of his buddies of what they'd done. And then, to twist the dagger he'd stabbed in her back, he also said she was lousy at sex." Inga closed her eyes and shook her head, and Caleb made a low, growling sound in his throat. "What a jackass. He completely ruined her life in Helena."

"What a little shit," Inga said of the young man. "Someone ought to teach him a lesson."

"So that's how I ended up with a new assistant to my secretary," Caleb said, his gaze distant, the anger he felt visible in his face.

Inga said in a voice barely above a whisper, "I was always surprised you turned your attention to me instead of toward her. She's so young. So young and beautiful and so lovely in so many different ways."

Caleb's palm was now resting lightly on Inga's thigh. He looked at Inga carefully, and she could feel his scrutiny.

"What is it?" she finally asked, uncomfortable with the silence in the room, especially when Caleb was looking up at her so seriously. "Ask whatever it is you're so curious about." She paused a moment. "I'll tell you the truth, no matter what it is."

"You talk quite often about how pretty Maggie is. Yes, I know she's pretty. I can see that. You can see that too, can't you? You can see it and appreciate it . . . because you've walked on that side of the tracks." His voice dipped seductively lower. "You've tasted those kinds of temptations, haven't you? Be honest. Tell me the truth."

She felt her pale cheeks become heated. She knew she was blushing furiously, and she knew exactly why.

Can I tell him the whole truth? The truth that I've never told anyone in my life? It was so many years ago and I was so young.

She cleared her throat two times, tried to speak and found she couldn't, then cleared her throat again.

Caleb said, "Perhaps, before you start, you should pour me a whiskey, and some wine for yourself."

She sat motionless on his thigh for several seconds, then she looked into his eyes and nodded. If she was going to tell the story of her life, a glass of wine in hand would help the process move along. Of that she had no doubt at all. Wine had a way of making a lot of naughty behavior less scary.

She stood. She was only a little surprised that her legs felt weak beneath her. She walked over to the cabinet where the liquor was kept and picked up the crystal decanter of Caleb's most-prized Tennessee whiskey. She poured three fingers' worth into a cut crystal lowball glass. For herself, she poured a smaller amount of wine into a glass. Though not a clumsy person, she was afraid she might drop the glasses as she crossed the room to Caleb.

How can I explain away my past? It happened so long ago. It's as though I lived in another world back then. Everything now just seems like a dream.

She handed Caleb his glass, then sat on his thigh again. She did not make direct eye contact with him. Out of the corner of her eye she watched as he took a hefty swallow of his whiskey. She took a swallow of her wine, then coughed a little. She didn't usually take swallows of wine, just small sips.

"Now tell me about her," Caleb said, his voice low but clear, his diction indicating a formal education, probably in New England, or somewhere in or near London. He was a Montanan, but he had spent much of his life away from Golden Valley. "What was her name? How did you meet her? I want to know everything about her—or at least as much as you're willing to share with me."

Inga took another sip of her wine to summon courage, then said, "I was young and attending boarding school, and she was the headmistress. She said she saw something in me that she didn't see in other girls and wondered if I might like discovering what that *something* was."

"Ah, yes," Caleb said softly, his smile charming and all-knowing. "That special something. One can only imagine how many knickers have fallen because of those words."

"The first time she kissed me, I was so scared I thought I was going to faint or maybe wet myself. But that feeling only lasted a moment or two. When the kiss deepened—when she put her tongue in my mouth for the first time—I didn't know what to do . . . but I knew that whatever the hell was happening was really kind of exciting. I knew it almost from the very beginning."

She suddenly realized that Caleb was once again caressing her inner thigh with his fingertips. He had been doing it before, but now that he was touching her intimately as she spoke of her past, his caress seemed more evocative, more electrifying. Though he hadn't touched her vagina yet, she could feel the pulse of her heart in her clit, and her nipples seemed so tight and erect that they almost hurt.

Memories of what she had experienced so long ago in that boarding house with the headmistress came rushing back to her, and she experienced once again—as though she was feeling them for the first time—the mysterious sensation and ecstasy of those erotic, frightening days of so long ago, when every experience was brand new, and it seemed to her that each one was more erotic than the last.

"The first time she kissed me, all the other girls were sleeping, but we were all in the same room. The headmistress—her name was Miss Abigail—kissed me for the longest time, the two of us standing there at the foot of my bed. Even though she kissed me for a long time, not a single kiss ever lasted very long. She was always stopping to look at the other girls to make sure they were still sleeping."

Inga closed her eyes, recalling those magical, mysterious events that had happened early in her life. Caleb's hand was now moving up her thigh, inching slowly closer to her pussy. The thought of stopping him from touching her intimately never even crossed her mind.

"She had her tongue in my mouth when she touched my breast through my nightgown for the first time. Even back then, as young as I was, I had the biggest bosom of all the girls." She felt herself blush a little more. "My entire life I've had the biggest breasts of every woman in the room. Always. It's a curse."

"You have," Caleb said softly, seductively, "the most magnificent breasts in the world. I swear to you that's true. I'm not just saying it because you're my lover. I'm telling you that because it's the truth."

It was the first time he'd used any variation of the word love with her, and the sound of it touched her in an intimate way.

She felt Caleb's fingers now at the very top of her thigh, a scant inch from the pulsing center of her passions—namely, her clit. She wasn't wearing knickers. She'd stopped wearing them when Caleb asked her if she would do without them for his convenience. She found it quite daring. From that moment forward, to be in public, appearing outwardly perfectly respectably dressed, yet knowing privately that she was without knickers, pleased her. Greatly.

Being without knickers added a certain excitement to being out in public which she hadn't anticipated. It was as though she was playing a game that the civilized world of Golden Valley—such civilization as it was—oblivious to. The awareness that she was mocking convention, that she was being naughty in the most impish of its meanings, delighted her to the core of her soul. Caleb had a way of making her feel adventurous . . . and once again . . . young.

"She touched my breasts for a while, but that wasn't enough, apparently, to give her what she wanted. She pulled my nightgown up and told me to raise my arms. Then she took my nightgown off. So, there I stood at the foot of my bed, completely naked with a dozen other girls sleeping in the room. I was shivering, but the truth of it is that I wasn't cold at all."

Inga watched as Caleb brought the crystal glass to his lips. He tilted his head back and drained the glass. The fiery look in his eyes was more intense than she'd ever seen it.

She took the glass from him and said, "I think you need a refresher."

When she stood, the skirt of her dress fell down again, Inga felt a sudden sense of safety. Caleb's hand had been dangerously close to her vagina, and Inga knew from experience that when he touched her most intimate and private place, she lost all ability to control her emotions . . . or her desires.

She refilled his glass. When she returned and sat on his thigh, she could feel herself trembling inside. She understood, instinctually as a woman can, that she was incapable of keeping secrets from this man. She also believed that she *didn't* need to keep those taboo truths from him because he *wouldn't* use them to harm her. This was a man who would always defend her, who would never fail in his duty to protect her.

She trusted him as she'd never trusted any man in her life. After her husband's betrayal, she thought she could never against trust any man. But then she never imagined a man like Caleb coming into her life. Actually, she'd never imagined there *was* a man like Caleb

"Continue with your story," Caleb said when Inga once again sat on his thigh. He pulled her dress up and put his hand on her leg. His thumb was at the exact place where her thigh joined with her pelvis and was so close to Inga's vagina that she inhaled sharply and for a moment held her breath. "Continue. She's taken off your nightgown so now you're completely naked. Then what did she do?"

"The unthinkable," Inga said softly, closing her eyes and wanting desperately to forget what had happened while knowing that she could remember every detail of that evening as though it was branded in her brain.

Chapter Seven

"At first, she just kissed my neck and my breasts. But then she bent her knees and kissed me lower. I could hardly breathe. The feel of her soft, wet lips against my skin was something that I'd thought about but never actually experienced." Inga closed her eyes for a moment. She could feel Caleb's palm on her leg. She had to moisten her lips before she could continue speaking. Her mouth seemed very dry. "It had felt nice when she was lightly pinching my nipples, but when she started licking on them, I had to bite my tongue just to keep myself silent. I didn't think that anything could ever feel so heavenly . . . but then she started sucking on my nipples and I realized that something could feel better. Much, much better. She went from one nipple to the other, then back again. As she was doing this, she was squeezing my bottom. Everywhere she touched me it seemed as though I became on fire."

Inga watched as Caleb took a hefty swallow of his whiskey. He looked up into her eyes, then down at her breasts, then back up into her eyes.

"How long did she do this?" he asked.

Caleb's thumb was at the top of Inga's thigh. She could feel her own lubricating nectar moistening the lips of her pussy. He was making her ravenous for the fierce lovemaking that he had taught her to crave over the past weeks. The more he loved her, the more she needed his fierce lovemaking.

She had to clear her throat twice before she could speak. "I can't tell you how long. It just seemed to go on and on, and the pleasure it gave me grew greater and stronger with each second. I think I could have stayed standing there, completely naked with a room full of sleeping girls, until morning. I didn't care if anyone was watching me, no matter how sinfully I was behaving." She shivered. "Actually, it might have been exciting to have been watched."

The last comment drew a half-smile from Caleb. Inga wondered if he thought her to be nothing but a foolish middle-aged woman who still fondly remembered something that had happened so long ago.

"I remember telling myself that I had to remain standing, no matter what she did not me, no matter what sinful pleasure she might introduce me to. It was a good thing I thought that because instead of caressing my bottom with both hands as she sucked on my nipples, she brought her hand around and slid it up between my legs. I thought I was going to die. I remember she said to me, "You're wet. I take that as a compliment." There wasn't anything about her that wasn't wicked."

She shifted her weight a little on Caleb's thigh. When she did, she felt the long, thick length of his erection pushing against her, straining against the prison of his exquisitely tailored trousers. His rigid cock let her know that he was finding her story about something she had done years ago to be very stimulating. The urge to rub her buns against his hard cock was overpowering, but still she resisted.

"Her finger slipped inside me so easily," she continued. "It went inside with no pain at all because I was so slick down there. Wet like I'd never been before." She closed her eyes and shivered. In a whisper she said, "Like never before."

She tried to take a sip of her wine. The glass was empty. She found it odd. She couldn't remember drinking the entire glass, yet she must have because the wine hadn't simply disappeared all on its own.

"Do you want to freshen your drink?" Caleb asked, his

voice husky with tension and just barely above a whisper. The timbre of his voice, though softly spoken, was astonishingly erotic to Inga.

"No. I shouldn't," she said, though she wanted more wine. She needed to blunt the sharp edge of her desire, and wine was the perfect instrument.

"It's okay to have another. This isn't a time for shouldn't." He laughed softly. "Actually, there's never a good time for self-denial."

She shook her head. The blonde spirals of her hair that ran down her temples danced against her cheeks. Inga could feel that her cheeks were warm. She could only wonder about how pink with embarrassment they must be.

She suddenly felt as though she were in a foreign, strange, dangerous place that she'd never been before. She wondered whether she should escape or play this scene of her life to the final act and curtain call. She put her faith and trust in Caleb. It seemed to her, at that moment, that her surrender was inevitable.

"I want you to know that I've never told this story to anyone. You're the first."

"And the last," Caleb said in a manner suggesting ownership.

She thought about what he'd said for a moment, then cast her questions away. She was determined to tell her story as completely and honestly as she could. She tried not to think too much about being thought of as a possession. Caleb inspired emotions that were new to her.

"Everything seemed so dizzying to me. I truly had no idea of what was really happening. The next thing I knew her tongue was playing with my navel. It tickled a little, and I remember wondering whether licking belly buttons was what other people did to each other. I didn't know. Back then, I didn't know anything at all. I was so naïve. So young and inexperienced. Everything was new and exciting."

"But you were learning, and learning fast . . . weren't you?"

To Inga, the sound of Caleb's voice was like a caress. It wasn't just oral, it was physical.

"She kissed my tummy, but not for long. She brought her hands to my bottom again, and I remember at the time being disappointed because her finger was no longer inside me, no longer pleasing me in that wicked way I had learned to enjoy so much."

Inga closed her eyes and brought her hand to her mouth. The next memory was vividly etched in her consciousness and would remain there for all time.

"And then she touched me with her tongue. Touching me with her tongue *down there.* I gasped at the shock of it. When I heard myself, I looked around quickly to see if I'd woken any of the other girls, but I hadn't. What I felt was amazing. When I looked down at my headmistress, she was looking up at me, obviously furious with me for having made such a noise. Then, slowly, her scowl turned into a smile, and she put a finger to her lips to remind me that I had to remain silent. Then she began licking me, softly and slowly, and it felt absolutely divine. And then—"

Inga's words were cut off when the tip of Caleb's middle finger eased between the lips of her pussy, then entered two knuckles' deep.

"Keep going," Caleb said, as though he wasn't doing everything in his power to make it impossible for Inga to speak.

"Then she stopped licking me. She started sucking on my clit." Inga closed her eyes briefly and gave her head a little shake. She was struggling to compose herself, but not doing a very good job of it. "I thought I was going to die. I'm not exaggerating. I thought I would die and go straight to hell for what I was letting happen to me."

"But you didn't die," Caleb said, moving his middle finger back and forth, pushing just a little deeper into Inga's slick, wet opening each time. "In fact, that headmistress of yours gave you a heavenly experience, not a hellish one."

"It was heavenly, and I didn't go to hell because of it. I had never felt anything quite like that, and it was only a few seconds later that I climaxed. I let out a scream. Three of the girls in the room woke up. As the headmistress distracted them, I got my gown back on. The headmistress was a very believable liar. She convinced the girls that I'd had a nightmare and that she had come rushing in to comfort me."

"Well, she may have been a liar, but she certainly did give you comfort," Caleb said, and Inga didn't like at all that he was making light of what she'd gone through that night so long ago.

"Don't tease me," Inga said. She sighed. "Your finger gives me so much pleasure. You know that don't you? Of course you do. You know my body better than I know it. Anyway, you certainly know how to please it better than I do."

"Let's get back to talking about the headmistress and her involvement in your life," Caleb replied casually, as though they were discussing figures in some business ledger instead of a lesbian seduction.

"The headmistress made it quite clear that she was disappointed with what had happened between us because I had been entirely on the receiving end of the pleasuring, and she had been left, in her words, unsatisfied and uncompensated."

Caleb chuckled softly. "Well, I've heard what happened to her called a lot of things, but never unsatisfied and uncompensated. But now that I think of it, the phrase seems pretty accurate." He withdrew his finger completely from her pussy, spent several seconds toying with her clit, then casually explained, "You've got to get to the end of the story. I won't let you climax until I've heard a full accounting of your youthful life of sin and debauchery."

A shiver went through her, part of it from the way Caleb had been caressing her so expertly, part of it because she could feel his pulsing erection against her buns, and part of it from the memories that were now coming to the surface of her consciousness after having been buried for so long. There was a time, it seemed to her now eons ago, when passion and the ecstasy that went with it were things she took for granted.

"After that I got called in to the headmistress's office quite often to be disciplined. Almost every single day I'd spend time in her office with the door closed and locked. We'd start out kissing and touching and things like that, but it was never long before she'd have her legs over my shoulders, and I'd stay there until she was satisfied with my performance. It was always her first and me second." Inga sighed wistfully. "Sometimes I wasn't even second. Sometimes it wasn't my turn at all. She must have been in her late forties or early fifties. I remember thinking her to be terribly old. I mean, she was attractive and all, but I was just a girl." She made a soft sound deep in her throat. "She maybe wasn't all that much older than I am now."

"How long did this go on?"

She smiled down into Caleb's shimmering blue eyes. "There's a twist to the story that I haven't told you yet." She reached down and put a hand on his wrist. "Stop that now. I can't concentrate on the story with you touching me like that."

Caleb moved his hand, so that his palm was once again on her thigh. He pouted, sticking his lower lip out theatrically. She almost giggled at his expression. She realized at that moment that she adored so much about the man. He carried so much responsibility on his shoulders, yet at times he could seem like a naughty schoolboy.

"After the first month, the headmistress summoned me to

her office. I thought I knew exactly what was going to happen but was I ever in for a surprise. With her in the office was one of my teachers. She taught Colonial American history. I would guess she was in her early twenties, maybe the middle twenties at the most. She certainly wasn't in her thirties." Inga felt her blush deepen at the memory of what had happened so long ago. "Her name was Miss Bradley, but in private I was to call her Madeline. She had brown hair and eyes, but very pale skin. She always kept her hair in a bun, just like I do, and she was always proper and dignified. That is, right up to the time she let her hair down, then she was someone completely different. It was as though there were two people inhabiting just one body."

"She was pretty?" Caleb asked.

She shook her head emphatically. "She wasn't just pretty, she was beautiful. Stunningly beautiful. At the time I thought she was the most beautiful woman who had ever lived."

"And you had sex with her?"

Again, she shook her head vigorously in negation. "I had sex with the headmistress, but with Madeline I made love. When things got started, the headmistress would insist that Madeline and I gave all our attention exclusively to her. She could be very selfish. She had the power, and she always made sure we were aware of that. So together Madeline and I would set out to satisfy her as best we could, pretending all the while that we weren't dying to be with each other."

"I think you're leaving out some important details." He raised an eyebrow to eke out more of the truth. He seemed to know there were many truths she could tell but thought she shouldn't.

"I remember Madeline and I were trying to fulfill our obligations to the headmistress when Madeline whispered in my ear, "Let's finish with this old hag so that you and I can concentrate on each other." And we did. We finished what we *had* to do, then we did what *we* wanted to do." She sighed. "Which, at the time, was each other." Another shiver of remembered ecstasy went through Inga. "She had the most beautiful breasts. They weren't oversized pumpkins like mine. They were just right. They were perfect. And she had the softest skin I'd ever touched. And her mouth . . . my God, her mouth. I could kiss her and kiss her and kiss her for hours and even if kissing was all that we did to each other, that would have been enough to satisfy me. But then . . ."

Inga grimaced at the painful memory. She raised herself up a little, then reached down. Her fingers, through the thin layer of expensive fabric, discovered that Caleb's impressive cock had lost none of its stature. She asked sincerely, "Doesn't that thing of yours ever go down?"

"Not when you're on my lap, and not when you're telling me stories like that," Caleb said through a grin. "Now let's find out if my mouth can be as entertaining as Madeline's, shall we?"

Firmly, he took her by the arms and lifted her, turning her at the same time so that she was half-sitting on his desk in front of him and still between his spread knees. When he looked up into her eyes, she could feel the fire in his soul. His gaze locked with hers as he began raising the skirt of her dress. It was as though he was challenging her to defy his desires.

"This Madeline woman has raised expectations," Caleb said as he pushed his chair back, then slipped down onto his knees on the floor in front of her. "I've got some serious competition. I hadn't expected that."

"No, you don't," she replied with a seriousness she truly felt. "You're one of a kind. You're the only one I want." She honestly meant that, too. "No one's better than you."

Caleb lifted his eyebrows as though he didn't quite believe what she had just said. She started to say that she was being truthful, that he was the only lover she wanted, but he had just raised her dress and chemise high enough to expose her sex. When he looked at her, his eyes widened, and he inhaled sharply.

He likes looking at me down there. She smiled at her reticence to even think naughty words, much less say them. *My pussy arouses him.*

She watched as Caleb slowly leaned forward. The desire she felt at seeing such a handsome and socially powerful man on his knees in front of her was intensely erotic. She felt coveted in a flattering way that she never had before. When he looked at her pussy like that, she felt like she was the most beautiful woman in the world.

First, he kissed her abdomen, then leaned back and looked up. She almost started to complain. She wanted a lot more kissing than just that. Caleb had taught her what she could expect from him.

He looked into her eyes and said, "Remember, you must remain quiet."

"I will," she promised. Then, unable to keep her wishes and words to herself, she said, "I want more. You sort of promised me that I could have more." She hesitated a moment, then said in a whisper, "Please?" She knew she sounded petulant and selfish, but he had taught her to want so much more than she'd had before in her life. "Please?"

There was a pleading quality in her Swedish accent that surprised her. Since she had become Caleb's lover, she had learned to crave the sensual delights that he could dispense with seemingly effortless ease.

Caleb turned his gaze down, paused a moment, then leaned forward and kissed the lips of her pussy. For several seconds he just kissed her very lightly, but then she felt his tongue ease between her sex lips. The pleasurable sensation his mouth gave her turned into something much more evocative. Instead of a contained campfire, she suddenly found herself having to deal with a forest fire that would soon become an inferno.

She watched and felt as Caleb used his thumbs to gently separate her petals to better expose her clit. She inhaled sharply through her nostrils and held her breath. She knew what wickedly exciting feelings were going to go through her within seconds. It was almost impossible to not sigh with anticipation. But she had promised silence . . .

She closed her eyes so that she could better concentrate on what she was feeling without the distraction of letting her voyeuristic tendencies have any influence. Limiting sensory input intensified it.

She felt his lips surround her clit, then shuddered when he sucked lightly on her. She flinched as the electric jolt of raw desire shot through her.

He's even better than Madeline, Inga thought, thinking of the young woman who had taught her so many wonderful things that polite people never speak of. Stifling a moan, she decided that Caleb was better, more skillful with his hands, lips, and tongue, than the lovely young teacher she'd known so many years earlier and had taught her so much. She hadn't thought that Madeline could be bettered . . . but she had been.

As Caleb sucked and tongued lightly on her clit, he eased a single finger between the petals of her pussy. She caught her bottom lip between her teeth to keep from moaning. She curled her fingers around the edge of the desktop near her hips and squeezed until her knuckles were white. It was difficult to continue breathing at anything that resembled a normal rate. Her heart was pounding.

She realized it had excited her to confess to Caleb of her licentious, lesbian experiences. She'd never before told anyone of what she had done back then, never spoken of the taboo pleasures she had embraced with all her heart and soul when she was in boarding school. But speaking of her behavior aloud made it possible for her to relive them again, not just in her mind, but with all her feminine senses that were receptive to wanton temptation.

She felt the tickle first. That initial tingling sensation which whispered that a climax was forming. But it was somewhere in the distance, the sexual fog that she could not see through though she could sense its presence. When Caleb inserted two fingers into her vagina as he continued licking and sucking on her clit with an artistry that she was just now discovering was possible, she thought she might fall to the floor. It took an act of willpower to remain in a standing position.

The approaching climax made its way out of the distant fog. She could see the orgasm clearly now. She could feel its building intensity, like a swirling tornado that tightens and tightens, spinning faster with each moment. Every second made its impending impact more intense.

She knew that tornadoes left destruction in their wake. She wondered how much would be left of her after she climaxed.

The eye of the storm. That's where I want to be. She smiled, but kept her eyes closed. *Caleb will take me there. He'll take me to the edge, then he'll push me into the abyss.*

In an oddly disconnected, lucid way, she realized that she was an incredibly lucky woman to have a lover she had such complete confidence in. She'd been married for years but she never once had confidence in her husband's ability to give her an orgasm when they made love. When she was sexual with Caleb, the first orgasm was guaranteed. Climaxes two, three, and four, and maybe even more than that, were always a possibility. Since taking Caleb into her heart, soul, and body, she never questioned *if* she would climax, only *how many times* she would.

As far as life's uncertainties went, she decided it was a nice one to have.

"Fuck," she whispered, using a word she didn't like to say, though sometimes it seemed to be the only one that was appropriate. This was one of those times. She was in waters she hadn't sailed before. "You're going to make me come."

Caleb's fist moved faster then, pumping two fingers into Inga as he sucked with increased vigor on her clit. The pulsing waves of orgasmic ecstasy that then fired through her almost frightened her. She clenched onto the edge of the desktop so tightly that if she had been holding someone's hand, bones most surely would have been broken.

When the multiple contractions finally subsided, and Caleb leaned back so that he was sitting on the heels of his boots, she looked down at him in utter amazement.

"You . . ." she said, then paused because her breathing, and her post-orgasmic emotions, were so volatile. "You could teach Madeline a thing or two about giving pleasure."

Caleb's smile reflected complete and total satisfaction. When she looked into his eyes, she knew she was seeing a man who simply loved pleasing her. Acidly, she also realized he had pleased many other women. Often.

"I think this is where I'm supposed to return the favor," she said quietly. She could feel herself blush at the statement. "It's time for me to get on my knees and stay there until you are just as satisfied as I am right now.

She felt as though Santa Claus was about to come down the chimney. She was about to get the best present anyone had given her.

It was then that there was a soft knock on the office door, and the sound of Maggie's voice threw ice-cold water on Inga's rather wicked hopes.

"Caleb, there's a Mr. Collinsworth here to see you," Maggie said from the outer office. "He says he has an appointment, and that it's very important for this appointment not to be postponed again." She seemed quite concerned.

"Damn," Inga said, now remembering Caleb's itinerary and all the obligations he had on a daily basis. He was a very busy businessman. He doled his time out very cautiously, and with an eye to professionalism.

"It's not your fault." Caleb rose to his feet, kissed Inga first on the nose, then on the lips. When he kissed her mouth, she could taste the juices of her own vagina on his tongue. She was embarrassed to find herself nothing less than scrumptious. "Duty calls. Damn, ain't that a bitch?"

Chapter Eight

Maggie wondered if Inga was displeased with her performance at work. Or maybe it was Caleb who was unhappy with the effort she was putting forward. All she was certain of was that she had been studying shorthand as diligently as she possibly could, but Caleb never commented on it.

And, of course, there was that part about Inga teaching her to be a better secretary, one that would please Caleb more. Whenever Maggie brought up the subject of needing instruction, Inga always said it would be sometime soon. But *soon* never seemed to happen. And it had been weeks now since Maggie had first brought up the subject. But day after day, when Inga went into Caleb's office, she did so alone, leaving Maggie on the outside, both literally and figuratively.

Maggie had taken to confiding in Inga, and though she found herself to be drawn to the older woman, she wasn't at all certain that the feeling was reciprocated.

She probably thinks I'm just a silly girl, Maggie thought, sinking into a kind of self-pitying mood that she'd been prone to since losing her virginity to a young man whose word of honor was worth nothing at all.

She tried to tell herself that Inga had always been a serious and attentive listener whenever Maggie decided to speak of her troubled past, but being a good listener wasn't enough to keep the gloomy moods away from Maggie's heart.

It had been an uneventful day so far at the office. Kimberly, Adam, and Bryce were off for the day, having decided to scout out the new casino and saloon that had just been built in Boulder City, and might be competition to the Cattleman's Emporium Saloon and Casino. It seemed to Maggie that the men she worked for were always wary of serious competition, even though everyone seemed to agree that Caleb's establishment was the one most preferred by the monied cattlemen in the territory.

If the dusty, unwashed cowhands of some of the other ranches wanted to wash the trail dust down their throats with cheap, watered-down whiskey, they could do it in one of the other saloons that catered to their crowd and charged for their whiskey—such as it was—at a price the cowboys could afford.

Maggie caught Inga surreptitiously looking at her. She'd been doing that more lately, and she wondered why. She tried to tell herself not to be insecure, but that was difficult. It seemed to her that, in the office, the secrets were aplenty, and she didn't have any of the answers. She didn't even have clues to the answers.

"You've said you want to learn how to make Caleb happy," Inga said, the sound of her voice jarring Maggie out of her troubling thoughts. "Do you still want that to happen? Still want a lesson in what it takes to please Caleb?"

The words sounded almost too good to be true, especially on a day like this one when her mind kept wandering into troubling territory and seemed to dwell on uncertainty.

"Oh, yes!" Maggie said quickly. "Oh, Inga, I want that so very much."

"In that case, your first lesson starts at five sharp." There was a cryptic smile on Inga's face that Maggie couldn't decipher. "Caleb likes his happy hour to begin at that time precisely, and not a second before or a minute after."

Maggie looked at the clock. It was a couple minutes to five. She'd have to wait for her first lesson.

There were times, during those minutes, when she could hardly sit still in her chair, or keep herself from checking the clock constantly. When she glanced over at Inga, she found herself often meeting the lovely woman's gaze.

She keeps looking at me, she thought with pleasure. *Maybe she's as interested in teaching me to please Caleb as I am to learn.*

She tried to concentrate on learning her shorthand, which both Inga and Kimberly were giving her lessons in every day. She wanted to be as good as they were. When they had a pencil in hand and one of the men was dictating, the pencils practically flew across the notebooks. Though she had learned all the symbols that signified words in shorthand, she wasn't nearly as fast and proficient as her coworkers.

She allowed herself to glance at the clock. It was a couple minutes to five. When she looked over at Inga, she once again discovered that she was being watched.

"It's almost five," Inga said in a soft, knowing tone. "And don't worry. I'm sure you'll do just fine."

"Do you really think so?" Maggie could hear the uncertainty in her own tone. "I really want to make him happy."

"I'll be there with you," Inga said. "You have to listen to what he and I tell you, and everything will be just fine."

"I'll do anything you ask me to," Maggie replied. "I promise. Whatever you say."

At precisely five o'clock the small bell on Inga's desk chimed. From inside his office, Caleb had tugged on the ornately embroidered bellpull, signaling that he wanted Inga to come into his private office.

Maggie's heart accelerated at the sound of the bell. She was finally going to get the lesson in how to please Caleb that she had been hoping for. She wanted to be useful, to be of real value to the man who paid her quite handsomely for her daily services.

"Let's go," Inga said, rising to her feet. "He doesn't like to be kept waiting."

"Just tell me what to do," Maggie replied with sincerity, bolting to her feet. "I'll do anything you say."

The smile that Inga gave her was one that Maggie couldn't quite read. It was subtle and sly somehow, with only the corners of Inga's mouth curling upward. And there was a light in the woman's blue eyes that Maggie couldn't really understand. She wondered if she just imagined that light. Though she was only eighteen, Maggie's keen mind realized that machinations were happening, and she didn't understand so much as half of them.

"Does he know I'm coming with you?" Maggie asked quickly, in a voice only slightly above a whisper. "He won't be angry with you when he finds I've come along?"

Inga stopped walking and turned toward the girl. She put her hands lightly on Maggie's shoulders and gave her a smile.

"He doesn't know that you're coming with me, but he and I have talked about this several times. He and I agreed that I would decide when the proper time was for you to extend your education."

Maggie was a little surprised when Inga leaned over and kissed her lightly on the cheek. It was an innocent intimacy they'd never shared before.

"Are you ready for your first lesson?" Inga asked, an eyebrow arched high above a crystal blue eye.

"I think so," Maggie replied. She inhaled deeply, then exhaled slowly. It was almost impossible to quiet her nerves. "At least I hope I am. Wish me luck."

Inga was silent for several seconds as she looked straight into the girl's eyes. She said, "I suspect you'll discover that luck has nothing to do with what's about to happen. It won't be luck, it'll be fate." She laughed softly and added, "You might even call it destiny."

Maggie realized clearly that she understood very little of what Inga had just said to her. What she was aware of, though, was that those words were of great importance to her, even if she didn't realize their full meaning.

Inga opened the office door, then stepped aside so that Maggie could enter first. Caleb was at his desk on the right side of the room. He had positioned his desk so that when the office door was opened, he wouldn't be immediately visible. Maggie suspected that the placement of his desk wasn't mere chance. Inga had warned her, almost from the very first day of her employment, that Caleb valued his privacy greatly. Maybe above everything else.

When Caleb saw her, his eyes widened, and the smile on his lips made her tingle inside with pleasure. It was the reception she had wanted but was afraid to hope for.

"I brought Maggie with me," Inga said, her Swedish accent slightly more pronounced than normal. "I hope you don't mind."

Caleb looked at the clock on the wall. His smile broadened. "For our five o'clock ritual? Of course not." He looked at Maggie and said, "Inga's been giving me reports on how you're coming along. She says your shorthand is improving every day. That pleases me. I suspected from the very beginning that you would be a magnificent asset to our economic endeavors."

Maggie had no idea how to respond, so rather than blurting out something that would cause her embarrassment, she said nothing at all.

Inga stepped up in front of Caleb's desk and said, "She's been very interested in learning how to please you, in discovering the things that I do which gives you pleasure. I thought this would be a fine day to give her an introduction into the way that the president of Cattleman's Emporium lives his life."

When Caleb turned his gaze toward her, Maggie felt as though she was being scrutinized. He rose slowly, unfolding himself out of his chair to stand at his full height. She looked at him and realized, at that moment, that he was much more handsome than she previously thought. She watched him carefully as he moved until he was standing directly in front of his desk. He half-sat on it, his well-polished boots in front of him and spread slightly, his black suit immaculate and finely tailored, the seductive smile touching his lips and hinting without words at improprieties Maggie suspected she shouldn't dwell too long upon.

But she *wanted* to think of those things.

Caleb looked at her and asked, "You're sure about this? You can walk out of the office right now if you want to and I'll not feel in the least bit slighted."

Maggie cleared her throat twice before she could finally say, "No. I want to stay." And then, after several seconds of silence where she simply looked into Caleb's eyes and took wonder at the power he held over the world they both lived in, she said, "Please let me stay. Please . . . teach me. I want to learn. I know you can teach me."

Caleb turned his gaze from Maggie to Inga and said, "Well, I gave her the chance to leave, didn't I?"

"Yes," Inga replied. "But you wouldn't have been happy if she'd left."

"You wouldn't have been happy if she'd left, either." He gave Inga a wickedly charming smile, and Maggie wondered what it meant. "Now admit that. Admit the truth that more than anything in the world, you wanted her to stay with us."

Maggie watched as Inga gave him an almost comically stern look, then said, "You're right. I wanted her to stay more than you can possibly imagine." She closed her eyes. "It was important to me. *She's* important to me."

"Then let's begin."

Maggie felt as though there were fingers surrounding her heart, and those fingers were slowly tightening into a fist. It seemed to her she was in invisible bondage. She was finding it difficult to breathe, and her mouth was dry as a desert.

"First things first," Inga said in a rather professorial tone. "Caleb is fussy about his libation, but it's very easy to make. Follow me." She walked to the one wall that had closet doors of brightly polished knotty pine and pulled one open. Inside, on a wheeled cart, were several bottles, and on a lower shelf there was a stack of crystal lowball glasses. "When you hold his glass, put three fingers around the glass, with your little finger beneath it. That way you'll know how much to pour."

Inga pulled the cork from a square bottle with a label on it. Maggie hadn't known that liquor bottles had labels. The only bottles she'd ever seen were just round, clear glass with amber liquid in them. Inga picked up a lowball glass in the manner she had just explained, then poured until the whiskey had reached the top of her first finger.

Caleb said, "That's not the second-rate whiskey we serve cowboys at the Cattleman's Emporium, and it's not the third-rate rotgut all the other saloons in Golden Valley sell." There was a noticeable current of pleasure in his tone. "That's genuine Tennessee sippin' whiskey. I save it for myself, and for some of my clients—men I like and respect as well as do business with."

Like a dutiful puppy, Maggie followed Inga back across the office to Caleb. She handed him the crystal glass. Caleb was looking straight into Inga's eyes as he first took a thoughtful sniff of the whiskey, smiled because of the aroma, then took a sip. After he did, he sighed softly with pleasure, then smiled warmly down at Inga.

"Now the first thing to do to make Caleb comfortable is take off his suitcoat," Inga said, and with a slight tilt of her head indicated she wanted Maggie to stand closer. It seemed to Maggie that Caleb was giving Inga all his attention. She wondered if he was even aware of her presence in the office.

When she was near Inga and there were men in the vicinity, Maggie felt she was practically invisible.

Caleb reached inside his suitcoat and from beneath his left arm he extracted a silver revolver with ornate engraving throughout its length. The grips were off-white.

Maggie's eyes widened and she said softly, "A silver gun with a pearl handle. I've never seen a gun look so expensive."

"Oh, it's expensive, alright," Caleb said as he placed the revolver on his desk. "But it's nickel-plated, not silver. And the handle is ivory, not pearl. Don't be fooled by its glamorous appearance. In my right hand it's as deadly as anything you can imagine."

Inga cleared her throat softly to direct Maggie's attention back to her.

"The first thing we're to do is start with his coat," she said, resuming the instruction.

The breath caught momentarily in Maggie's throat when she watched Inga slide her hands inside the black garment. She was clearly caressing Caleb's chest through his silk shirt. After several seconds, Inga eased the suit's shoulder off Caleb. She waited as he took another her sip of his cocktail, then shifted the drink to the opposite hand. Carefully and sensually, she got the garment completely off Caleb.

Inga crossed the room, and on a thick wooden hanger, hung it up on the coatrack. When she crossed the room to return to Caleb, there was a slight sway to her hips which Maggie suspected hadn't been there earlier.

"Now you remove his shoulder holster," Inga said, speaking to Maggie though her gaze never once left Caleb. "This has to be hung up, but not on a hanger." When she returned from the coatrack, there was a shining quality in her ocean blue eyes that hadn't been there earlier. "Now pay attention because this is very important to Caleb. Once he's at this stage of relaxing, you start with his necktie." Caleb tilted his chin slightly upward, and Inga loosened the necktie's knot. She slid the necktie from beneath his collar. "And unfasten the first two or three buttons of his shirt." She looked at Maggie, gave the girl a seductive half-smile, and in a significantly softer voice, said, "This is where life in this office gets interesting." In a normal tone she said, "You must undo his cufflinks, then fold each cuff upward toward his forearm twice."

Inga took Caleb's left wrist in her hand, raised it, then brought his hand to her left breast.

Maggie gasped. She couldn't help herself.

Inga continued to hold Caleb's hand to the fullness of her bosom. Maggie watched as Caleb's fingers intimately pressed into the lush mound. For a moment Inga's eyes closed, and her lips parted with pleasure. After a full thirty seconds, she removed the gold cufflink from Caleb's shirt. He continued fondling her breast through her clothing while Inga finished her task.

The process was repeated with the other cuff. Watching Inga's extravagant breasts being casually fondled caused Maggie's breathing to quicken considerably, and she felt her own nipples tighten and become sensitive, even though they weren't being touch.

"Now he's comfortable." Inga turned to face Maggie directly. She reached out and gently eased a tendril of blonde hair that had come loose from her coiffure and tucked the strands delicately behind her ear. "Let's sit on the sofa so we can all discuss that foolish young man you were with who said such awful things about you."

Maggie's jaw dropped open and she said, "You promised me you wouldn't tell anyone. You made that promise to me."

Inga eased her hand into Maggie's and squeezed affectionately. "Caleb is the exception to the rule. I suspect you'll find that he's the exception to *every* rule. Come now, let's sit together on the sofa and see what we can do to make sure that we never again hear rumors about you not being skilled in the art of lovemaking."

Chapter Nine

Inga didn't have to drag Maggie over to the sofa, but it was clear that the girl wasn't overjoyed with the thought of sitting with her.

In a whisper, Inga said, "Just do what I tell you. Everything is going to be just fine. You'll see. You've just got to trust me."

Maggie felt her heart pounding in her chest. She was utterly furious that Caleb now knew her life's most intimate—and embarrassing—secrets.

"Sit down now," Inga said, patting the seat cushion. Maggie did as instructed, but Inga gave her a stern look. "Closer than that. Your hip should be touching mine. And put your arm around me."

Inga leaned forward, and when Maggie put her right arm behind her, she leaned back quickly so that Maggie's arm was pinned between her back and the sofa. Inga then put her left arm around Maggie's slender shoulders. The tips of her fingers were lightly touching Maggie slightly above her left breast. Maggie felt the awareness that she was slowly walking into a trap.

"That's better," Inga said. "Now put your hand in mine. Turn your wrist so that we are palm to palm and our fingers are laced together."

Maggie complied with Inga's orders, and she found immediately that she no longer had the use of either hand. She felt herself to be in invisible bondage. She found it unexpectedly erotic.

"Don't be frightened," Inga said, her voice a seductive purr. Her face was so close to Maggie that she could feel the warmth of her breath. "Look into my eyes," Inga whispered, lightly stroking Maggie's face with her fingertips. "Don't be scared. The first thing you must do is kiss me like you kissed that young man who doesn't deserve to look at you much less take possession of your beautiful body."

But you're a woman, Maggie wanted to say in protest.

She didn't, though, because a moment later Inga's lips were brushing lightly against her own. After a few seconds, Inga's head began to move as the kiss became firmer, more intense. Maggie tried to free her left hand from Inga's, but she found that she couldn't. When she tried to move her right arm, Inga simply leaned back, and in doing so, more securely trapped the arm between her back and the cushion.

Maggie turned her face away and breathily said, "Inga, I don't think—"

"That's right. Don't think," Inga said quickly, clearly in no mood to let Maggie protest for very long. "Now I'm going to kiss you again, and this time I want you to kiss me back."

Inga turned Maggie's face toward her. Inga's eyes were open when she was kissed a second time, more firmly and intimately than before. She felt Inga's hand slide from her cheek to around the back of her neck. She heard Inga moan softly as they kissed, and Maggie realized that even if she herself was nervous to the point of being frightened, those certainly weren't the emotions that Inga was experiencing.

But Maggie was aroused as she'd ever been in her life. She couldn't admit it . . . but she couldn't deny it.

From a dozen feet away, while still half-sitting on his desk, Caleb said, "Beautiful. Watching the two of you kiss is so amazing. I've never seen anything so erotic."

The sound of Caleb's deep voice brought back the reality to Maggie that she wasn't alone with Inga. The handsome and mysterious man she worked for was standing nearby, sipping a cocktail—and watching as Maggie was scandalously kissing a woman who was two decades her senior. In her mind, the age difference was suddenly by far the lessor transgression.

Inga ended the kiss and looked into Maggie's eyes. There was a glassiness in Inga's eyes that hadn't been there just moments earlier, and Maggie suspected that what was shining in Inga's eyes was lust.

Have I inspired that?

Maggie was afraid of finding out what the true answer really was.

Maggie heard words being spoken. Words in a feminine voice. It took several seconds before Maggie realized that she was the one who had uttered them.

"Will you kiss me again?" she heard herself ask, the undercurrent of begging beneath the surface but still there nevertheless. She could hear it. "I promise I'll do better next time."

Inga kissed her again, more firmly and intimately than before. When Maggie felt Inga's tongue touching her lips, she hesitantly opened her mouth, separating her lips only a little. It was enough acquiescence for Inga. She slipped her tongue smoothly between Maggie's lips and into her mouth. When she did, a shiver of delight zipped up her spine.

She had heard about kisses where tongues went from one mouth to the other and back when she was in Helena and her girlfriends shared stories. Only a small portion of those tales were actually true. What was happening to her now was so true it was something akin to a living fantasy.

To feel Inga's tongue exploring her mouth was intensely, vividly erotic. She squirmed. She tried to free her hand from Inga's gasp, but she failed. Inga had her pinned to the sofa and had made it impossible for her to use her hands to defend herself. Maggie felt powerless and defenseless . . . and the combined sensations made her clit throb with tension and the lips of her pussy swell and moisten with anticipation.

Her defenselessness was a euphoric narcotic that was as scary as it was thrilling.

Their tongues danced, Inga's with skill and long-remembered experience, and Maggie's clumsy with inexperience but filled with youthful exuberance.

I never knew a kiss could make me feel this way. After a few seconds she asked herself, *Why didn't I know that until now?* She felt as though there were pleasures she should have experienced but hadn't because of the person she was with.

She smiled, knowing she was no longer with the person she had been with . . . and the man and woman she was with now would explain to her the answer to the mysteries in life that had confused and confounded her.

Maggie felt Inga's palm resting lightly on her cheek move slowly, the fingertips gliding across the surface of her skin, sending a trail of heat through her blood. When Inga's fingertips reached Maggie's throat they hesitated briefly. After several seconds they continued their downward journey.

Maggie was sliding her own tongue into Inga's mouth when she felt for the first time a woman's hand close over her breast and squeeze firmly. Billy's hand had never elicited those types of feelings.

A tremulous sound came from Maggie's throat. It was a small squeak of fear and excitement and the sexual unknown all jumbled together. The sound matched her emotions perfectly.

Once again, she tried to free her arm from where it was trapped behind Inga. She tried . . . but she didn't try very hard. She didn't have her heart in the effort. Not when Inga had made her nipples so fiercely erect and was taking turns pinching one nipple and then the other through her chemise and dress.

Maggie turned her face away again, unable to breathe it seemed while she kissed Inga with steadily building passion. When Maggie stopped kissing Inga, Inga simply transferred her attention to the girl's throat.

Maggie had never felt warm and wet lips sensually come in contact with her neck. When Inga sucked lightly on her throat, the experience was electrifying. Maggie felt herself losing control of her own emotions.

"Oh, God!" Maggie gasped, her slender body shivering on the sofa. "That's . . . that's . . ."

Maggie's passion-addled brain could not come up with a proper word to describe what she felt. She opened her eyes, afraid that by keeping them closed she might discover that this was all just a beautifully erotic dream. But when she opened her eyes, she found herself looking into the eyes of the most seductively gorgeous man she'd ever met in her life. He gave her a warm, lazy smile, and while looking into her eyes, took a small sip of whiskey. He was a man entirely at ease with the eroticism occurring around him.

It's exciting that he's watching me.

The awareness shocked Maggie, but only a little. She knew she'd always liked being on stage.

Maggie angled her head a little more to the side, intentionally giving Inga greater access to her throat, which Maggie now realized was sinfully susceptible to stimulation. It irked her that she'd never realized it until now. Someone should have taught her before this moment, but no one had. Not until Inga.

Maggie let her eyes close. She was slightly disappointed when Inga stopped squeezing and toying with her breasts. A moment later, though, when she felt the cloth buttons of her dress getting unfastened, starting from high near her neck and working swiftly downward, Maggie was only too delighted. Inga's fingers seemed very skilled at the task.

Inga kissed her neck again, even as her deft fingers unfastened the buttons of the girl's chemise from the top to the bottom, near Maggie's navel.

Inga used the backs of her fingers to slowly separate Maggie's chemise to expose her pert, young breasts. Maggie sighed into Inga's mouth. She felt herself being consumed by a desire, a passion, that she'd never before experienced—or even knew was possible.

"Your breasts are so beautiful," Inga whispered, her pupils dilated with desire, her free hand trembling slightly. "There isn't anything about you that doesn't inspire passion."

She captured Maggie's nipple between her forefinger and thumb, pinched, then gave the nubbin a slight twist. Maggie gasped in both discomfort and delight. This was so much more than she would have imagined was possible. She felt as though she was crossing into a new world.

"You have sensitive nipples," Inga said, a touch of triumph in her tone. "I always suspected you would. And you would like me to suck on them. Breasts as beautiful as yours simply have to be treated with the proper respect."

"Oh, God," Maggie whispered softly, keeping her eyes closed. She felt herself lost in emotions beyond her comprehension.

"Trust me, I'm not God. Not even close." She let out a soft sigh and said, "Though I try to be heavenly. It's a worthy goal, don't you think?"

Inga started to bend forward to take Maggie's tempting nipple into her mouth, but the instant she released the pressure of her back against the cushion which kept Maggie's arm trapped, the girl tried to escape. Inga instantly tossed herself backward, once again imprisoning Maggie's arm, keeping the girl defenseless against a feminine seduction that was both devious and delightful.

"Caleb," Inga said sharply, "it appears I'm going to need some help with Maggie in learning her lessons. Would you please show her how a man kisses, and when you done with her first lesson, I believe her nipples need some sucking on." Inga chuckled softly. "Actually, I'm absolutely certain that they need to be suckled." She paused a moment, then said,

"And they look quite delicious."

Maggie didn't know if she was living a nightmare, or a dream come true. She was squirming, but not actually fighting against the hands that held her securely. Her breath was coming in ragged gulps. The lips of her pussy were practically drenched in lubricating cream. She was quite more than ready to get fucked.

"Wait," Maggie said with absolutely no sincerity. The last thing she wanted was for Inga to stop what she was doing.

"When it comes to pleasure," Inga said, her eyes alight with mischief, "there's never a reason to wait."

Maggie looked at Caleb. He was impossibly tall and handsome and everything that she could want a man to be. He was also immaculately dressed in clothes that could only have been hand-tailored specifically for him. And in his trousers, quite noticeably, was an erection that desperately needed to be set free.

There was a significant difference, Maggie realized, needing nothing more than a glance, between what Billy put into her and what Caleb rather obviously wanted to put into her.

"Oh, God," Maggie whispered, though she strongly suspected that deities really had nothing to do with what was happening in her life at the moment. Actually, she hoped deities weren't paying any attention to her at all. She was quite certain she didn't want the scrutiny.

"Kiss me," Caleb said, putting his knee on the cushion of the sofa. "I've been wanting to taste your lips since the first moment I saw you."

From the first moment?

It was a dizzying thought for Maggie. She felt intimate parts of her body clench at the awareness. She watched as Caleb moved nearer. She closed her eyes. She felt Inga pinch her left nipple with just the right amount of pressure to draw the maximum amount of pleasure. Was it feminine intuition that she knew what to do without having to be told?

"Oh, God," Maggie whispered again, though she wasn't at all certain she wanted God's scrutiny to what she was doing right now.

She might have said more, but then Caleb's mouth was over hers, his lips stealing away her breath. All coherent thought simply vanished from her mind. She couldn't think. All she could do was feel.

And that was just fine with her.

Maggie opened her mouth without hesitation. She wanted Caleb's tongue exploring deeper, and that's exactly what she got. Immediately. And feeling Caleb's tongue caressing her own was a sensation that Maggie found erotic in the extreme.

Maggie felt herself responding to Caleb's kiss in ways she never anticipated. She could feel the lips of her sex swelling, becoming more puffy and moist, and her clit both tightening and elongating.

She swirled her tongue against Caleb's. The feel of his mustache was prickly, and though her initial reaction to it was negative, this response very quickly changed in the extreme. His mustache, the feel of it against her mouth as he kissed her deeply and hungrily, represented masculinity in its most elemental manner. She responded to his manliness instinctively and profoundly, and as she sucked on his tongue, she realized that whenever Billy kissed her, her body had never reacted at all like this.

As Caleb kissed her deeply and passionately, Inga brought her mouth to the side of Maggie's throat. For Maggie, to be kissed on the mouth by a gorgeous man as a beautiful woman kissed her neck was very nearly more than she could consciously comprehend. She moaned, softly and soulfully, into Caleb's mouth.

There wasn't a nerve in her body that wasn't wickedly, wildly aroused. Her clit literally ached with the need of attention and stimulation. It was a sensation she had learned to crave.

"Her nipples," Inga said in a quiet voice that held with it sexual tension. "Suck on her nipples. I . . . I'm not in a position to."

Caleb ended the kiss with Maggie, and she had the instantaneous sense of suddenly having been deprived of something that she wanted very much. She felt like a child who had been given a surprise gift that had suddenly and inexplicably been taken away from her.

Her disappointment did not last long because Caleb moved lower on the sofa, opened his mouth wide, and sucked the crest of Maggie's left nipple between his lips. He sucked quite hard. There wasn't an action he made that wasn't masculine in the extreme.

Maggie was immediately aware of the warmth and wetness of Caleb's mouth but also of the scratchiness of his mustache against her sensitive skin. She was looking at him as he feasted on her body, and Maggie was consciously aware of the fact that she'd never seen anything quite so erotic as Caleb's handsome face pressed tightly into the delicate, pale mound of her breast.

But there was something special about the feel of his mustache . . . .

Inga put her hand once again to Maggie's face, forcing the girl to turn toward her. She kissed Maggie firmly, with feminine, not masculine force, thrusting her tongue into the girl's mouth. Maggie swirled her tongue against Inga's, shivering now in her awakening acceptance of feminine pleasure that could only be administered by a confident woman in full bloom.

She felt Caleb release her nipple, and she was about to complain since she was now greedy for the desires her body was capable of feeling. But before the words could escape her mouth, she felt Caleb kiss her stomach as he slid off the sofa and knelt on the floor between her wide-spread knees.

"Oh, no," Maggie whispered as Caleb's powerful arms slipped around her thighs from the underside. He hoisted her legs over his broad shoulders.

She watched as Caleb brought the tips of his fingers to the pink lips of her pussy, gently separating them to more completely reveal her clit. First, he just flicked his tongue against her, but then he sucked her clit between his lips. When he did, Maggie's mouth opened wide. She arched her back, pressing her pussy more firmly against Caleb. The experience, unprecedented, made Maggie feel as though her body was burning from the inside out.

Maggie tried to keep her eyes open to watch what was being done to her, but she couldn't. She turned her face toward Inga and was instantly greeted with a soul-searing kiss that delighted every responsive nerve in her body. When Inga pinched her nipple, then firmly twisted and tugged on it, the pleasure-pain Maggie experienced was electrifying.

Don't stop. Don't ever stop. Do to me whatever you want. I'm yours to have however you want me.

Nothing in Maggie's limited sensual experience could prepare her for what was happening. She felt herself go from the verge of panic to complete ecstasy. And it all happened in a blindingly fast period of time.

Maggie felt as though she should say something to protest what was being done to her. She was in sexual and emotional territory miles and legions beyond anything she'd ever before dared to wander. But whatever words she wanted to say wouldn't form in her mind, and it didn't really matter anyway because Inga was kissing her mouth with an ardent desire that thrilled every nerve in Maggie's body, and Caleb was licking her like she was the most delicious piece of candy in the world. She couldn't possibly speak coherent words.

This must be how Heaven feels, Maggie thought, though she hadn't before given much thought to what it was like in

Heaven.

She felt Caleb's lips—complete with the world's most erotic mustache—press again against the lips of her pussy, and the word *fuck* screamed loud and clear in her mind, though she did not speak the obscenity because she was dancing her tongue against Inga's, and she couldn't soulfully French kiss a gorgeous woman and shout naughty words of praise at the same time.

She felt Caleb ease a single finger between the lips of her pussy as he sucked her clit between his lips. The pleasure she had previously experienced was eclipsed by a factor of ten an instant later. She wrenched her face away from Inga's, and though her mouth opened wide, and her entire face contorted into a grimace, as though she was in pain though quite the opposite was true, she did not emit so much as a squeal of sound. A better judgment she hadn't known she possessed had warned her to remain silent.

Then her body began contracting, twisting and turning while continuing to be securely held by Inga and Caleb. The spasms were fierce, almost—but not quite—painful in their intensity. The contractions came in waves, the first one the most powerful of them all, and the four that followed it, each decreasing in intensity, though each satisfying, nevertheless. She held her breath throughout them all. She simply could not breathe throughout the tumult.

Once the last contraction had worked its way through her body, Maggie could take no more of the pleasure that Caleb was providing.

"S-Stop," Maggie heard herself say, her voice barely audible. Instinct told her that silence and secrecy were critical. "Please . . . I'm begging you. Please stop." She made a sound in her throat that was almost a whimper of despair. "I can't take any more." And then, with great sincerity, she asked, "What the hell was that?"

CHAPTER TEN

Maggie had to blink her eyes several times before she could clear her vision. The surface of her skin tingled. From head to foot, her skin felt as she was receiving low-voltage electrical current—even now, after her climax. Never before in her life had she felt anything like what she had just experienced. What had just happened eclipsed everything else.

But if there was anything that she was certain of, it was that she wanted whatever the hell had just happened to happen again. Soon. And not like something *this month* soon. More like *nobody leaves this room until that happens again* soon.

What in hell just happened to me.

With her chin nearly touching her chest, she looked down at her body. Her breasts were exposed, her nipples and areolas moist with saliva. Caleb had sucked on them. The memory of it caused a slight shiver to work its way up her spine. Her dress and chemise were in a heap just beneath her navel. Her pale, slender legs were still up on Caleb's shoulders. He was looking at her with an expression in his dark eyes that Maggie wasn't certain she could interpret accurately. His lips were shiny with her own lusty nectar. To see it on Caleb's mouth seemed both obscene and wantonly delightful. She wondered what he thought of her receptiveness of the pleasure he seemed so willing to give her.

"Darling girl," Caleb said, then turned his face to the side and kissed the inside of Maggie's tapering, naked thigh. "That was the first of many, many orgasms that I intend to give you.

And just so you know, you're delicious. Absolutely, positively scrumptious."

Inga said, "You have me at a disadvantage. It's been decades since I've tasted a beautiful girl. Too many years. I've probably forgotten how to do it properly." She chuckled throatily, lustily. "But I intend to make up for lost time with Maggie."

"I . . . I don't know what I'm supposed to do," Maggie said in a whisper. "Nothing like this has ever happened to me before."

Caleb once again kissed the inside of Maggie's naked thigh only this time he bared his teeth and gave her a little bite. She flinched. He chuckled.

"Inga and I will teach you everything you need to know." His chocolaty eyes were alight with mischief, and the dimple in his cheek suddenly seemed particularly deep and boyish. "It'll be an education that'll never end. There will always be something more to learn. You never actually know everything, but it's important that you try."

"It's not a destination you get to and then stop," Inga said, stroking her fingertips along Maggie's cheek as she spoke. When Maggie tried to slip her hand out of Inga's, Inga wouldn't let it happen. "It's a lifelong journey . . . and the three of us are going on it together." To Caleb, she said, "I think Maggie should find out what it feels like to have a real man inside her. Be gentle with her, Caleb. She's new to all this. Why don't you release that beast you've got in your trousers? I'm sure she's more than ready for her next lesson in lovemaking."

Maggie squeezed Inga's hand, but she did not ty to free herself. It seemed to her so utterly bizarre that Inga and Caleb were making all these critically important decisions of her life without asking for her opinion at all. And most of the time when they talked, they did so as though she couldn't hear them or know what they planned to do with her.

Caleb rose to his feet, and to Maggie, he seemed to be a giant of a man. She watched his fingers carefully as he unbuttoned his shirt and opened it to reveal the triangle of hair that went from his chest down to his navel. He pulled the shirt's tails out of his trousers but left the shirt on.

Look at how broad his chest is. The hair makes him seem powerful, manly. The muscles in his stomach . . .

Her thoughts regarding Caleb's naked upper torso abruptly ended when Caleb unbuckled his belt. Maggie first watched his hands, but then her gaze drifted slightly lower, and the bulge in the fabric was ostentatious.

Maggie let out a small gasp and said to Inga without taking her gaze away from Caleb's concealed erection, "He's so . . ."

"Isn't he though," Inga said with humor in her tone.

Caleb did not hurry as he unfastened the buttons of his fly. Maggie could tell that he was a man who had been gazed upon lovingly by countless women as he undressed himself for their voyeuristic pleasure.

He's so confident in himself, in his charms, Maggie thought. *I don't think I'll ever be so sure of myself.*

But she hoped she would. She wanted it very, very much.

Caleb unknotted the drawstring of his drawers, then released the three buttons of his fly. Instantly, his erection—very long, extremely thick, and more than just a little bit frightening to look at—sprang out. Maggie's breath caught in her throat. The idea that he was to put *that* into her made Maggie embrace nervous doubts as to whether such an act could ever be a source of pleasure for her. She had her doubts.

Caleb lowered his trousers and drawers, but only to the tops of his thighs. Maggie could feel the heat of his gaze as he looked at those parts of her body which were exposed. She inhaled deeply, and though she was certain it wasn't possible, she thought she could smell his desire for her.

Caleb sank slowly to his knees. His cock was jutting

straight out from his body. The skin over the crown seemed stretched so tautly that it would split. A blue vein ran a squiggly path along the broad, upper surface of the shaft. Maggie could see Caleb's racing pulse in that vein.

Inga said, "Easy now. She's not used to you."

She's protecting me and seducing me at the same time.

It was a comforting thought for Maggie to have, and her estimation of Inga increased significantly because of it.

Caleb took the shaft of his erection into his hand. He stroked himself several times before he rubbed the conical head against the delicate lips of Maggie's sex.

Maggie was looking down, between the quivering mounds of her breasts, at the cock that was about to push into her body and—at least for a period of time—become a part of her.

It'll never fit. He's too big.

"It'll be divine," Inga whispered, as though she could read Maggie's mind. "I was a little concerned myself the first time I saw him, too. But he's masterful. Trust me."

Maggie's body was still tingling from the afterglow of the orgasm that Caleb's wickedly arousing mouth had given her, and though the sensation had subsided somewhat, when she watched and felt as Caleb rubbed the crown of his cock against her clit, then up and down over her sex lips, she felt her desire once again heightening, the warmth in her veins heating as her heart began beating faster and faster.

Inga tried to kiss Maggie on the mouth. Maggie would have none of it. She turned her face sharply away and said, "Don't. I want to watch him."

Inga kissed Maggie's temple, then courteously moved out of the way.

Maggie watched as the head of Caleb's cock pushed between her pink lips. He moved forward very slowly. As delicate flesh was forced apart, Maggie's jaw clenched, and her lips pulled back in a grimace. It wasn't blinding pain that she felt, but she certainly wasn't accommodating Caleb without discomfort.

He hadn't quite forced the entire crown into Maggie before he started his slow withdrawal. When he had retreated entirely, Maggie breathed in and out several times very quickly, and she stopped grimacing. Once again, temptingly, Caleb worked the knob of his erection up and down over Maggie's entrance, and this time he paid special attention to her clit, which was now throbbing with Maggie's youthful spirit and anticipation.

Then Caleb was pushing forward again, and Maggie was opening for him. He advanced in a powerful and yet measured way. He did not stab. Maggie wasn't ready for that kind of lustful exuberance, and Caleb seemed to understand that. Maggie watched as the crest forced her lips apart, then disappeared within her. She gasped softly. Her mouth opened. What she felt was a combination of prickly pain and a mysterious sense of being connected to a man who had the power to turn something that was bad into something that was delightfully, erotically, inexplicably . . . magnificent.

It took Caleb six revolutions of his hips before he had buried himself completely inside Maggie's sweetly receptive sex.

"Does," Maggie said, then had to lick her lips to moisten them before she could go on, "it always feel this good?"

"I'll try to make it so," Caleb said as he grinned roguishly, then leaned forward so that his chest was pressing against the girl's breasts. "Each and every time."

When he kissed Maggie, she could taste her own juices on his lips. It was a delicious reminder of what he had done to her. Once again, his mustache tickled and aroused her. His mouth claimed hers, and his tongue caressed hers with consummate skill. She'd never known that a kiss could be so exquisite. She felt her vagina clench in response.

Caleb eventually leaned back on his heels and the instant he did, Inga moved to the side and kissed Maggie passionately, her tongue wickedly and instantly seeking and then receiving entrance. To Maggie, it was supremely erotic to go from kissing the most masculine man she could imagine, to a second later sharing a kiss with the most ostentatiously feminine woman she'd ever known. The differences between Caleb and Inga were factors that made being with them—together, at the same time—so arousing.

Caleb began pumping his hips in earnest, sliding his erection to the hilt into her until his pelvis collided with hers. Each time this happened, Maggie let out a little cry of ecstasy. When he was deep inside her, she felt filled to overflowing with his masculinity. She went back and forth, first being kissed by Caleb, then receiving the feminine version of that from Inga.

Maggie began to wonder how long Caleb would last. With the only other lover—though she realized *lover* was not the correct word to use regarding Billy—she had never had to take more than a minute and a half of his exuberance. Caleb had already been making love to her much longer than that, yet it seemed as though he was nowhere near ejaculation.

Maggie was just thinking about how wonderful it felt to have Caleb's sizeable sex seesawing back and forth between the lips of her pussy . . . when she felt that strange and delightful sensation begin again deep within her trembling body. She had only felt that feeling once before, and that was earlier that day when Caleb had driven her to insanity with his lusty kisses to her clit—which had never been pleasured by a talented mouth before.

She thought she should tell Caleb that he mustn't ejaculate inside her, but she couldn't get her throat to form the words. And mere seconds later she whispered "oh, God" and experienced vaginal contractions that took control of her body, causing her to wrestle against the hands that held her securely, and the gorgeous man who continued pumping into her throughout her wrenching climax.

She was just coming to the end of her mysterious and blindingly erotic experience when Caleb let out a groan. He withdrew from her completely and unleashed a series of powerful eruptions that left four rivers of sperm from her chin to her belly button.

"Oh . . . my . . . that's a lot," she said, looking at the warm cream on her body. When she looked at Caleb's handsome face, she saw that he was breathing deeply. In his dark brown eyes was an expression of unutterable delight, and she felt wonderful about that.

Inga released the hold she had on Maggie. It surprised her that she didn't feel in the least bit jealous that the man she loved—and she now accepted love as a fact and not just wishful thinking—could dispense his amazing sexual skills on Maggie, and Inga didn't feel so much as a twinge of jealousy.

"Caleb, you've made one hell of a mess," Inga said, a smile on her lips. "But you always make one hell of a mess, don't you?"

She looked at Caleb's cock. He still had half an erection, but even only semi-erect, he was still much more than almost all men. His cock was shiny from Maggie's juices and looked about as delicious as a filling meal as Inga could conjure.

Inga leaned forward on the sofa so that she no longer had Maggie's arm pinned behind her. When she looked at the girl, she noticed that Maggie, with a curious expression on her face, was looking at that part of Caleb that had given her so much pleasure.

"What is it, darling?" Inga asked softly. Thinking she might need a confidence boost, she said, "You were wonderful."

Maggie nodded in the direction of Caleb's cock. "He didn't shrivel. Whenever Billy ejaculated, he shriveled immediately to almost nothing."

Inga chuckled softly, knowingly. "You've got a lot to learn about Caleb, don't you? And I've got to improve your vocabulary. I haven't heard a girl use the word *ejaculate* since I was your age—and that was a long time ago."

Inga got off the sofa. When she looked down at the girl, she felt saliva form in her mouth as though she was anticipating a delicious meal—which, in a way, she was. The creamy lines of come on Maggie seemed both lurid and enticing, and Inga had to stifle her more uninhibited desires. She knew what Caleb's come tasted like.

"You made her a mess," Inga said with mock censure in her tone, "so it's your responsibility to clean her up. Now take out your handkerchief and clean up after yourself."

With a low, throaty chuckle, Caleb took a handkerchief from his pocket and got down on one knee to wipe the semen he had deposited on Maggie's young, delicious-looking body.

As Caleb cleaned, Inga was busy removing her own clothing.

Throughout this encounter, Inga had mostly been a spectator rather than a participant. She intended to change that lamentable condition post haste.

When Inga had removed her chemise and she was completely naked, Maggie uttered a small gasp and said, "Your breasts. They're so large . . . so big and beautiful. I'm puny compared to you." She sighed. "You make me feel not pretty."

Wiping away the last of the semen from Maggie's navel, Caleb said to Maggie, "Never discount your own beauty. Your breasts are beautiful, too, just in a different way."

A small shiver of erotic delight went through Inga when she heard the compliments that were being directed at her. She couldn't deny that she harbored doubts and insecurities because of her age, but her dramatic hourglass figure was something she was proud of. And it seemed Caleb was pleased with her.

"Now it's my turn to have some fun," Inga said as she got down on her knees in front of Maggie. "Caleb, come to me and let's see how fast I can make you go from half-mast to raging flagpole."

"Again?" Maggie exclaimed, her jaw dropping open. "But he just—"

"Don't say *ejaculate* or I'll bite your nipples hard enough to make you squeal. What Caleb just did was come. And it was a doozy of an orgasm, but he's a long way from being finished with us." Inga reached out, took Maggie by the hand, then tugged. "Come closer, darling. Get down on your knees beside me. Let me teach you something you need to learn."

Maggie resisted, but Inga was not going to let the girl's inexperience and inhibitions prevent her from learning skills that would be critical as the three of them progressed with their lives together.

With Inga's assistance, Maggie was soon completely naked and on her knees beside Inga and in front of Caleb. Inga wrapped her fingers around the shaft of Caleb's cock. She stroked him several times. She could feel the blood flowing into the shaft. Her man was swiftly growing harder, thicker, and longer.

Whispering directly into Maggie's ear so that Caleb wouldn't hear, Inga said, "You'll want to learn how to do this. He loves it. He loves it a lot. And often. Most often every day."

She kissed the crown of Caleb's cock several times, then licked it before taking it between her lips and into her mouth. She used her tongue against the underside of the crown and was delighted when she heard Caleb groan softly. She felt his erection reach its full, magnificent stature in less than a minute. Inga continued bobbing slowly, and as she did, she reached with her left hand between Caleb's legs and cupped his heavy testicles in her palm.

"That's so damn good," Caleb said. "Magnificent. Absolutely the best." Inga's confidence soared when she heard what Caleb thought about her oral skills. She sucked on him for a full minute before she sat on her heels and released him. She turned to Maggie and, while angling Caleb's cock toward the girl, said, "Now you do it." She saw the uncertainty in Maggie's eyes. She suspected the girl had never even thought of sucking a man's cock, much less actually having done it. "Watch me again, then you do it." She winked at the girl. "By the way, I can taste you on him and I think you are delicious."

Inga took her lover deep into her mouth an instant later, not stopping until the cockhead was pressing against the opening of her throat. Her mouth, quite literally, was completely filled with his lusty flesh. With her mouth full, and Caleb being far too large to take down her throat, Inga rotated her face and squeezed his balls as she stroked that part of the shaft that was in excess of her capabilities.

"Yes, yes, yes," Caleb said, his tone soft and deep. "You're amazing, Inga. Simply, spectacularly amazing."

Inga once again released Caleb. She turned to Maggie and in a low voice said, "You've got to at least try to please him." She kept her voice soft enough so that only Maggie could hear her. "Please?"

Inga watched as Maggie, hesitantly, leaned forward and planted a chaste kiss on the head of Caleb's cock. Just as Inga was about to seriously consider that Maggie simply couldn't summon the courage to open her mouth wider, she watched as the girl took the entire crown into her mouth. It seemed as though she had been uncertain at first but had finally made up her mind to be bold.

But hardly had Maggie taken as much of Caleb's cock into her mouth as she could when Caleb let out a startled gasp and pulled back instantly.

With her lips close to Maggie's ear, Inga whispered, "All lips and tongue, but no teeth. That's very important to remember." She looked up at Caleb and added without whispering, "She'll get better as we do this to you more often. She'll get better, I truly promise." Then she kissed the pulsing knob of Caleb's erection and declared with confidence, "She'll get better, and I'll be the one to teach her."

For the next ten minutes Inga and Maggie remained on their knees, and Caleb continued standing. The women passed his cock back and forth selflessly, sharing Caleb's bounty. Each time Maggie took the hard erection into her mouth, Inga could see that the girl was doing better at giving pleasure with her lips and tongue and was avoiding any unpleasant contact of teeth that created quite the opposite reaction she was hoping for. Inga felt herself to be a suitable teacher, though she knew there was much more sexual wisdom she needed to impart.

Maggie sucked hungrily on Caleb's cock, her cheeks caving inward as she drew a firm suction. Inga tilted her head back on her shoulders, looked up into Caleb's gorgeous face, and said after releasing Caleb, "This is good. But I need more. I need to feel you inside me, and I want to taste Maggie at the same time."

Once again, Maggie had to be seduced into doing what Inga wanted her to do. But Inga realized it was all part of the game of life and lust. Maggie's reticence acting as an aphrodisiac that heightened the pleasure of the seduction. It took some gentle kisses and soft caresses for Inga to get Maggie seated back on the sofa where she had been earlier. Inga was on the floor between the girl's spread knees. When she inhaled deeply, she caught the unmistakable aroma of feminine arousal. This pleased Inga enormously. She wanted the girl to be thrilled with what was about to be done to her . . . and it seemed she was.

"It's going to be beautiful," Inga whispered as Caleb got down on his knees behind her. It had been twenty years since Inga had tasted the unique flavor of a girl's passion. She hadn't realized until that moment how much she missed it. "I want you to come. I want you to come on my mouth, just like you did for Caleb." She felt the bulbous crown of Caleb's erection begin spreading the lips of her slick cunt, moving into territory it had been many, many times before since he'd become Inga's lover. "Fuck," Inga gasped, looking into Maggie's eyes as the cock began stretching her.

For the next ten minutes Inga experienced the unprecedented thrill of having her gorgeous male lover fuck her from behind while Maggie, her new and lovely young female lover, trembled and shivered as her pussy was licked and sucked and fingered with a skill that Inga had thought she might have lost over the years of neglect. Inga realized now that the experience that a woman needs with her lips and tongue to please another woman had come back to her with crystal-clear clarity. And she was only too happy to dispense her skills.

Maggie was the first of the trio to climax, her beautiful eyes as round as saucers as she looked at Inga throughout the jolting orgasm. Inga was next to come, reacting as much to the excitement of tasting Maggie's young pussy as to taking Caleb's ramrod thrusts. When Caleb pulled out of Inga and unleashed another torrent of come, she felt the first eruption splatter her from the back of her head to the small of her back.

It wasn't the first or even second time she'd had his semen in her hair.

CHAPTER ELEVEN

Kimberly looked at the clock on the office wall and felt a sudden sense of fear and doubt. She knew she still had time to change her mind, to alter the direction of her desires. Instead, she embraced her own courage and sense of daring.

To Inga, she said, "I've got to walk around for a bit. My legs are getting stiff. You don't mind, do you?"

"Of course not. The men are up to their eyeballs in paperwork," Inga replied. "If anything comes up, Maggie and I can take care of it."

Kimberly glanced at the clock once more. It was two minutes to three. She had been looking at the clock every few minutes for the past several hours.

She crossed the room, inhaled deeply to bolster her courage, then stepped out of the office and onto the walkway that overlooked the most famous saloon and casino in all of Golden Valley. She went to the railing and looked down at the gamblers. It was a normal crowd for this time of the afternoon. It wouldn't become a raucous crowd until seven or eight. Her eyes were open, but she really wasn't seeing anything.

"I'm here," a female voice said, speaking just loud enough to carry to Kimberly.

Kimberly turned and looked at the woman who had spoken. Her name was Molly. She was petite and pretty and fun to talk to. No one looking at her or talking with her would guess that she was what was known as a Second Floor Girl at the Cattleman's Emporium. She was a few years younger than

Kimberly, and she sold her passion to men who could afford her prices and treat her with respect. Her prices were high because she was in high demand.

A floor-to-ceiling railing, identical to those used on the handrailing of the stairs leading up to the second floor, separated Kimberly from Molly. A man couldn't go from the second-floor ladies' rooms get to the door leading to the offices of Caleb, Adam, and Bryce.

Kimberly looked around quickly. Was she being watched by anyone? She tried to appear nonchalant but didn't know if her effort was succeeding. When she was on the second-floor balcony, there weren't many people who couldn't see her from the first floor.

"Hi, Molly," Kimberly said, looking into her new friend's eyes. "Did you bring it?" There was tension in her voice.

"Would I let you down?" From a purse she extracted a small, velvet bag. She handed the bag to Kimberly. "Do you remember everything I've told you?"

"Everything." Kimberly squeezed the velvet bag. She could feel there were two objects inside. She tried to quell her fear, but she couldn't. She wanted to feel brave, but it wasn't the emotion she felt in her heart.

"You're sure you don't want me to help you? At least the first time?"

Kimberly sensed that Molly wanted to be with her, but she had other plans. She was determined to do this alone, though she sympathized with Molly's disappointment.

"You're going to make some man very happy," Molly said. "You tell him how lucky he is. He's being given a priceless gift. You're sure you won't let me help?" When Kimberly shook her head, Molly gave her a look of disappointment and said, "Then at least you should let me know his name." Kimberly held out a gold coin, but Molly shook her head. "You don't need to pay me. I'm your friend and I want to teach you things that I've learned. Things you should know." She paused a moment and repeated, "I'm your friend."

"I'd better get back to my desk. Thanks, Molly. I owe you a favor." She felt a little guilty, though she couldn't quite understand why.

Kimberly took a sip of her wine. It was a hearty red zinfandel from California. She was naked in her room, and on her third glass. She was sitting cross-legged, and on the floor in front of her was what Molly had explained was a Queen of Spades. It wasn't a playing card. It was clear glass, though it was shaped very much like a spade in cards. The base was round and flat, then the glass narrowed significantly before swelling outward until it reached its maximum width midway to the top. But the glass object did not have a sharp, pointed tip like a spade. Instead, it was gently rounded. It had no sharp edges or points to it at all. If it did, it would be dangerous. Its purpose was esoteric. And erotic.

Next to the Queen of Spades was a tin box. Kimberly had removed the lid and had already used the ointment on herself. Setting her wine glass aside, she dipped two fingers into the ointment, picked up the Queen of Spades, then slathered ointment onto the precious object everywhere but on the base.

Molly said to use lots of ointment, and to go slow. Molly knows best about these things.

Shifting positions so that she was now on her knees, she took another sip of wine—only this time it was more of a gulp than a sip, and she emptied the glass before setting it aside. Then, very slowly, she rose up several inches. She positioned the Queen of Spades directly beneath herself. She lowered her hips until she felt the carefully rounded tip of the glass touch the virgin entrance of her bottom. She stopped lowering her hips.

She said to go slow. Be patient.

She thought of stopping, and then told herself not to be a coward. She had invested too much emotion into this journey to turn back now.

She lowered herself a fraction of an inch. The tip of the glass, smoothly rounded and heavily lubricated, pushed into her bottom a very short distance. It didn't hurt, though it did feel strange. She lifted up, and the glass slipped out of her completely. Kimberly began to think this was going to be easier than she had feared.

So far, so good. Now take more of it.

The second time she lowered her hips, more of the Queen of Spades pushed into her taboo passage. The glass was getting rapidly thicker. She felt something more than just a twinge of pain. When she raised her hips, the sensation of the glass sliding out of her bottom gave her a sense of relief. And pleasure. Her mind was in a whirl. Pleasure. Pain.

How the fuck did those things become intertwined? More next time. Not all of it, but more of it.

She did take more, and the glass getting thicker and thicker, and stretching her ass more and more. She thought about abandoning the quest, then cursed herself for giving the thought any consideration.

The next time she lowered her hips, she felt the glass slide into herself until it was at its thickest. She felt more than discomfort—it hurt. To have her bottom being forced to expand as much as was necessary was outright painful.

Don't stop. Take it all.

She lowered her hips another fraction of an inch. Quite suddenly she was at the base of the Queen of Spades, where it was very narrow, but the base was flat and round and not meant for insertion. Once the glass was completely inside her with the exception of the base, the pain stopped, almost as though it had never happened. The difficult part, the moment at which it was most painful, was where it was thickest. She had gotten it all the way in . . . but now she had to get it all the way out. She understood that she had started something she couldn't stop.

That awareness was a little frightening.

She was sitting on the floor with all but the flat base of the glass in her ass. With a hand that was shaking only a little, she poured wine into her glass, filling it to the rim. She brought the glass to her mouth and drank greedily. Some red wine trickled from the corner of her mouth and dripped onto her white breast. She took a second and then third swallow, set the glass down, then slowly and carefully lifted her bottom off the floor. Her sphincter tightened. The glass did not move from its position inside her. She rose to her feet, her ass tightly squeezing the Queen of Spades. She took several steps.

Yes, everything is exactly as Molly said it would be.

The awareness didn't surprise her. If there was anything she understood, it was sex . . . in all its variations.

Standing, with her feet spread, she reached behind herself and caught the base of the glass between her thumb and her first two fingers. Her breath was coming in ragged gulps. She pulled the glass out of her forbidden place. Once again, the thickest part hurt the most, but only momentarily. Almost immediately, she pushed it back in. The pain, this time, wasn't what it had been the first time.

For the next two hours Kimberly drank wine and pushed and pulled the Queen of Spades. What had initially caused her nothing but pain had in time caused her clit to become stiff and her pulse to quicken with excitement.

While continuing to push and pull the glass in and out of herself, she reached between her thighs. When she touched her pussy with the tip of her middle finger, she found that her clit was fiercely erect, and the lips of her pussy were puffy and slick with nectar. She pushed a finger into her vagina. It slid in easily. She began using both hands to pleasure herself—one to work the glass in and out, and one to massage and caress her clit.

When she climaxed, she fell to her knees and screamed of her ecstasy.

Later on, she hoped the neighbors in her hotel didn't hear her. She hoped no one had, but the truth was she really didn't care all that much one way or the other. She was basking in the afterglow of her climax, and nothing other than that truly mattered much.

Three days later, Kimberly had the outer office to herself. Caleb had taken Inga and Maggie with him to the cattleman's convention in Helena, traveling in Caleb's private rail cars. They would be out of the office for two days. Kimberly had big plans for what would happen in those two days.

She looked at the clock. It was five o'clock. She locked the door leading to the outer office, then began unbuttoning her blouse. She undressed completely, tossing her clothes into an untidy mess onto her desk. When she was completely naked, she knocked on the door leading to the private office of Adam and Bryce. Her heart was pounding against her ribs. She had never before been this bold.

"Come in," she heard Adam call out. She'd never once heard his voice when it didn't please her.

Kimberly opened the door, then stood in the doorway for several seconds, enjoying the shock on the faces of the men she was about to get ravaged by.

"I've locked the outer door," she said as she walked to the center of the room. "There are no more appointments. We won't be disturbed. I'm yours to have . . . any way you want to have me."

The men rushed at her, and she raised her arms in greeting . . . or was it submission? Adam kissed her mouth fiercely. His need was intense, and she could feel it. As she took his tongue in her mouth, she felt Bryce begin sucking hungrily on her nipples. The pleasure was electrifying. One of the men—and she wasn't certain which one—put a hand between her legs and started rubbing her pussy vigorously. Hours earlier, just thinking about this moment had caused her cunt to get hungry. When a finger was thrust between the lips of her pussy, it entered smoothly.

Oh, yesss. They know. They know how to do it exactly the way I want it.

The men took turns kissing her. Their hands never stopped moving over her body, pinching and tugging on her nipples, squeezing the cheeks of her ass, thrusting fingers into a pussy that was so wet with passion her cream almost dribbled down the insides of her thighs. She felt overwhelmed in a way that brought her nothing but pleasure. She wondered if she could die from so much ecstasy.

Adam put a hand to one of Kimberly's shoulders, and Bryce on the other. Together they pushed her to her knees. They practically tore open their trousers to get their passion-swollen cocks out.

"Oh, yes. This is what I wanted to—"

The words were cut off when Adam shoved his cock between her lips, not stopping until the crown was pushing threateningly against the entrance to her throat. She couldn't take any more of what he had to give. Adam held her tightly, not letting her retreat. She started to squirm on her knees and was on the verge of gagging when Adam finally released the pressure one second before Kimberly had reached her limit.

The relief she felt once released went to the marrow of her bones.

"Now me," Bryce said, pushing Adam's hand off her head. He grabbed her by the hair and began fucking her mouth an instant later. He wasn't gentle with her. She had known these men wouldn't be easy or gentle. And they most certainly wouldn't be passive. They were men who dominated life, and to assume they would be different where sex was concerned was an act of folly.

As Bryce slipped his cock back and forth between her lips, Adam undressed hastily, tossing his clothes to the office floor. When he was naked, he stepped forward and rubbed the head of his cock against Kimberly's hollowed cheek as she continued sucking on Bryce.

"Let me have some of that," Adam said. "We've got to get her to the sofa. I want more than just her on her knees."

Perfect. Exactly as I had hoped. A shiver went through her. *Now I'm really going to get fucked.*

Another shiver went through her when she realized she had started something that she was powerless to stop.

The men sat on the sofa while she sank to her knees between them. The frantic nature of their initial coupling became a little less uncontrollable. As she sucked one cock she stroked the other. She tried to give the men equal attention because she didn't want one to think she adored the other more.

She sensed that the ice beneath her was very thin.

"I want your pussy."

It was Bryce who had made the bold statement. Between her lovers, it was always Bryce who was more demanding of her, more barbaric with her. She rose to her feet, turned her back to Bryce while he sat on the sofa, then positioned herself above him. She lowered her hips and reached down to guide Bryce's cock to her pussy lips. When she felt him press against her opening, she moaned softly, deep in her throat.

Bryce took her by the hips and pulled her down, impaling her deeply. Tossing her head back she felt the shocking sensation of her pussy being forced open wide.

The awareness of having Bryce's cock inside her was nothing less than exquisite.

Adam got up from the sofa and moved so that he was standing directly in front of her. She raised her hips, then lowered herself until the cock inside her was buried full-length.

She was pleased that Adam waited until she was properly positioned. He was a barbarian . . . but a considerate one.

Looking up at Adam she said, "Fuck my mouth."

He did. Hard. She thought he was behaving more like Bryce than himself. She now understood they were both Alpha males. She felt herself to be nothing less than blessed.

Kimberly bounced and sucked. Her heavy breasts jiggled and swayed. In the back of her mind, she realized that she had always needed two men—specifically, these two men—though it had taken some time to realize what she now considered an undeniable fact.

She put her hands on Adam's hips, indicating that she wanted him to stop filling her mouth with his enormous erection. She made a soft sound of disappointment in her throat when she was suddenly and completely emptied of cock.

It's time to take the next step. This is what I prepared myself for.

This time, when Kimberly lifted her hips, she raised herself high enough to get Bryce's cock completely out of her pussy.

"Don't worry, Bryce, I'm not done with you. You're going to like what happens next," she said as she reached down and guided the head of his cock to the entrance of her ass. "We've got to take this slow and easy. I've never done this before. You'll be my first . . . and Adam will be my second . . . eventually."

He's a lot bigger than my glass Queen of Spades. This is going to hurt.

She told herself to relax, but when she felt Bryce's cockhead pushing against her ass, she involuntarily tightened up. She couldn't help herself. It was a natural reaction.

This isn't going to happen. He's too big.

Bryce put his hands on the rounded curve of her hips and pulled down. She gasped loudly when the crown of his erection pushed beyond her resistance and drove into her bottom. She felt a sharp bite of pain as her ass was forced to stretch more than it ever had before. And Bryce was not a man of diminutive dimensions.

"Wait. Wait," she said rather frantically. She only had half of Bryce's cock inside her bottom, but already she felt filled to capacity. When Bryce stopped pulling her down a wave of gratitude washed over her. She suspected most men wouldn't have such discipline or decency. "Just give me a few seconds . . . some time to adjust. This isn't as easy as I thought it would be." She groaned. "You're very . . . thick."

She straightened her knees a little, pleased that Bryce allowed her to retreat, and was thrilled at the sensation her sensitive bottom felt when the thick, hard cock slipped slowly out of her. The sensation was a weird combination of relief and pleasure. She could only guess what the next sensations would be.

As though it was someone else speaking, she heard herself say, "Let's try it again."

Bryce's fingers tightened on her hips. He pulled her down slowly, his iron-hard cock spreading the cheeks of her ass, forcing them slowly but steadily wider apart. He impaled her forbidden passage with nearly the entire length of his erection. She lifted, and the next time he pulled down on Kimberly's hips, he didn't stop until the cheeks of her bottom were against him, and every pulsing inch of his cock was inside her. She felt his cock get even harder. It was a staggering awareness for Kimberly. She hadn't thought it could be possible.

"I've done it. I've taken everything he's got," she whispered, speaking the words as much to herself as to the men. To Adam she said, "Okay, now you can have my mouth again."

She bounced on Bryce as she sucked hungrily on Adam. Then, with the cheeks of her ass spread wide because of Bryce, she looked up at Adam and said, "Fuck me." This was her wildest fantasy, and she could hardly believe that she was going to live it out. Her emotions were in complete turmoil. "I want both of you inside me at the same time."

Instead of continuing to lean forward, as she had been, she leaned back. Adam wasted no time getting into position. He put one foot on the floor and one on the seat cushion as he brought the knob of his cock to her glistening, moist cunt. He pushed forward slowly but with strength. She felt the lips of her pussy adjusting to his dimensions. She had to stifle the urge to scream.

Adam was very thick. When he penetrated a woman, her private parts were forced to accommodate.

Seconds later, Adam was working his cock into her rapidly overheating pussy with long, smooth strokes. The feeling of having two cocks inside her body at the same time was almost overwhelming. She could feel Bryce beneath her. He was trying to move, but with her weight on him, and with Adam's weight much of the time also on him, his ability to drive upward was greatly hindered. But he was still solid as a rock, and he was buried deep inside her tush. She was vividly aware of every inch of him.

Her back was against Bryce's chest and Adam's cock was pumping between the lips of her pussy when she felt the climax approaching. She sensed that it wasn't far in the distance. It was quite close when she first became aware of it, and it was getting nearer with each jarring invasion of Adam's cock.

"Fuck . . . me," she said between thrusts. "Hard."

It was almost impossible for her to realize that she had just spoken those words.

Adam responded exactly as requested. Several seconds and many furious thrusts later she began to come. Her pussy and ass contracted around the hard men that filled them. The orgasmic convulsions were more powerful than any that she had ever before experienced. Wave after wave of pure emotion washed over her with the impact of a tsunami against the shoreline.

The spasms had just stopped when Adam withdrew completely. He stroked himself and streams of thick, creamy come splattered Kimberly's perspiring body. His body, leanly muscled like a panther, glistened with sweat from the energy he had put forth to please her.

"I thought I . . . was going to die," she finally managed to say between deep gulps of air. She looked up at Adam, who was standing now, his gorgeous body glistening wetly with perspiration. "That was amazing."

From beneath her, she heard Bryce say, "You're a long way from being finished."

What happened next was a feat of strength and agility that was so amazing she could hardly believe it. Bryce shifted his weight slightly, then sat up on the sofa without ever once becoming dislodged from her. For a moment he was just sitting on the sofa with Kimberly's weight on his thighs. Then he put his arms around her middle—arms thick with muscle that held her like a vice—and stood up.

Her mouth opened in shock, but no sound came out. Bryce held her with her back against his chest, his cock buried deep in her tush. Her bare feet dangled more than six inches off the office floor.

He's going to fuck me to death. There's nothing I can do to stop him.

Then Bryce twisted sharply and lowered her onto the sofa. She was flat on her stomach lengthwise on the cushions, with Bryce on her back. Throughout the entire move, she had his cock inside her bottom.

Her legs were together and his were on the outside of hers. He suddenly seemed very heavy as he pressed her into the cushions of the sofa. She could feel the heat of his ragged breathing against the side of her face on one cheek, and the comparative coolness of the leather seat cushion on the other side.

What happens now?

She wanted to ask the question, but she couldn't get her throat to form the words. The cock in her ass seemed to have grown to astronomic dimensions.

Her arms had been above her head, but Bryce pulled them down until her hands were at her sides near her hips. He licked the circumference of her ear with the tip of his tongue, then flicked his tongue into her ear before biting softly on her earlobe.

"You're so exciting," Bryce whispered. "Too exciting for words. The sexiest woman I've ever known."

He began moving his hips. Slowly at first, but with steadily increasing tempo and energy. At first Kimberly was capable of taking the downward plunges without a powerful reaction, but soon she was literally bouncing on the sofa. Each time Bryce's body came in sharp contact with the rounded cheeks of her ass, she gasped as the breath was forced from her lungs.

Soon the sound of a perspiring pelvis coming in fierce contact with the cheeks of a woman's ass echoed off the walls of the office. Bryce pushed his fingers into her ebony hair and pulled her head back on her shoulders to bare her neck. When he kissed her throat, it was with an intense combination of teeth, lips, and tongue.

Kimberly felt like she was being eaten alive.

She'd never experienced anything like this. This was in a reality all of its own. She was being driven into the cushions of the sofa with great force. The sound of flesh striking flesh was exhilarating to her.

"Love," Bryce said.

I didn't expect that, she thought, her eyes closed as a soft smile began curling her lips. *I didn't expect that at all.*

Chapter Twelve

Maggie tried hard to concentrate, but it wasn't easy. She had the pencil in her hand and was doing her shorthand while Caleb dictated. She showed sufficient speed and accuracy—but concentrating on the words he spoke was a herculean task, and one she was hardly up to.

"Please be confident that this venture between us will be highly profitable," Caleb said, the tone of his voice authoritative and not in the least bit anything other than professional, "and that together we will forge a future we will both be proud of—oh, damn, that feels so fucking good—and will be of great value to our—you're so fucking incredible—communities."

Maggie's pencil moved rapidly over the page as she took shorthand dictation from the man she worked for and loved with all her heart and soul. She was in his office and sitting on his right thigh.

"Did you get all that?" Caleb asked her.

"Yes," she answered, "though I edited out the words of praise you had for Inga."

"As well you should have," he replied. "Your good judgment is beyond your tender years."

The smile he gave Maggie while she sat on his knee warmed her heart, and other parts of her body somewhat south, which were irrationally responsive to such stimuli. She wanted to kiss him then, though she did not. Her discipline remained intact, though not without great effort. She felt her nipples harden.

"Is there anything else?" she asked.

"Just the usual conclusion. Sincerely, Caleb Essex, President, the Cattleman's Emporium Company, Golden Valley, Montana."

"Of course," Maggie said, then finally turned her gaze down from Caleb's handsome face to the beautiful woman who was on her knees in front of him, sliding her soft lips back and forth over a cock that was long, thick, and throbbing with lust. "Is there another telegram you have for me, or is it my turn to be on my knees?"

Caleb's smile touched Maggie simultaneously in both her heart and clit. For a moment she found herself unable to breathe normally, and she felt a shiver of marrow-deep lust go through her. There wasn't a nerve in her body that wasn't vividly alive. She could feel herself getting wet.

"Let Inga take shorthand," Caleb said after a moment of hesitation. "You don't mind taking over for her, do you?"

"Never," Maggie replied without a second's hesitation. "Never ever. I promise you that's the truth."

Inga rose to her feet, a dreamy smile on her lips. When Maggie looked at her, she thought once again that she, Maggie, was the luckiest girl in the world to have the affections of a man and woman like Caleb Essex and Inga Olafson. She closed her eyes when Inga kissed her on the cheek, and then on the forehead.

"Have fun," Inga said in a whisper as Maggie began sinking to her knees to take Inga's place in front of Caleb.

"I will," Maggie replied in a quiet voice. "And so will he."

Maggie settled to her knees. As she did, she purred softly, like a kitten would with an empty stomach when sitting comfortably in front of a bowl of warm milk.

Maggie watched her fingers curl around the thick shaft of Caleb's cock. He was slick with saliva because only moments earlier Inga had him in her mouth. It mystified her that she didn't feel in the least bit jealous that the man she loved had just been getting his cock sucked by another woman—but that was only because the *other woman* was someone Maggie also loved.

Caleb's voice was deep and melodious as he resumed dictating. Maggie registered in her brain that the telegram was to someone in the federal government, and that it had something to do with renewing a contract for providing trained, tamed riding horses for the cavalry.

As Caleb's voice drifted into her ears, Maggie leaned forward and pushed her lips over the crown of his cock. She moved slowly, sliding her lips over an erection that she knew from experience was extremely sensitive to what she did with her tongue. When she held the entire head of Caleb's manhood in her mouth, she put her tongue in motion on the underside. When she did, she felt him flinch because he was so responsive there.

I'm getting better at this, she thought with a sexual self-confidence that was new to her. *He groans and moans more with pleasure when I've got him in my mouth. In the beginning, he didn't do that very often. Now he does.*

With an assuredness she previously lacked, Maggie took Caleb to the back of her mouth, then rotated her head as her tongue got even more busy in giving him delight. From above her, she could hear that Caleb was dictating the next telegram to Inga, but she paid the words little attention. It was the sound of his voice that pleased her, that aroused her.

After several seconds, she pulled up, once again very slowly so that he would precisely feel the contact of her soft lips against his hard cock. When she held only the tip of his knob between her lips, she tongued the slit. Once again, she heard him moan with the ecstasy she provided. He had to clear his throat several times before he could continue dictating the telegram to Inga.

He's never asked me to swallow his come. I wonder if he'll want me to this time.

The thought surprised Maggie. She had been told by Inga that Caleb's sperm didn't taste what any woman would think of as something delicious, but that over time it became something tolerable, especially when she saw the look of gratitude in Caleb's eyes when she swallowed.

In a voice hardly more than a whisper, Inga said, "Maggie is so beautiful . . . when she's on her knees with you in her mouth."

Maggie waited for a response from Caleb, and when none came, her insecure heart skipped a beat, and she wondered if his opinion of her being on her knees was significantly different than Inga's.

"What?" Caleb asked, his voice a passion-husky groan of sound. "Oh, yes, we were talking about the Finnermann contract, weren't we? Yes . . . that was it . . . Maggie can be extremely distracting."

Maggie felt Caleb place his hand at the back of her head. He pushed downward, gently and not forcefully, allowing Maggie to take him as deeply into her mouth as *she* wanted, not how deeply *he* wanted. She purred with contentment, loving the man who could either be dominating or lovingly gentle, depending upon the circumstance . . . and his whims and wishes.

"I've got to be the luckiest man in the world," she heard Caleb say, his voice so low she could hardly hear what he said, though the honesty of his emotions rang clear and true with every word. "What did I ever do to deserve the two of you?"

And I'm the luckiest girl in the world to be on my knees in front of you.

Maggie suspected she'd never had a more honest thought in her life. She drew a firm suction on his cock, and moaned softly with the delight she took in pleasing this man.

Kimberly looked up into Adam's eyes and said softly, "Promise me that you'll kiss me forever and forever and always. You kiss divinely.

"Yes," Adam said, and to emphasize his honesty, he squeezed her left breast through her dress and chemise. "I will kiss you until neither one of us can breathe. I'll kiss you until our lips are numb."

"I think I'd like that," she said. "I think I'd like that very much." She shivered, then added, "Promise me again."

There was a certain desperation in her tone that she heard, and she didn't like it at all, though she couldn't deny its existence. But she did want his kisses. She wanted them with all her heart and soul, and everything that she held dear to her heart . . . but she didn't want to admit to that.

She didn't want to appear needy.

Unless . . . it was with Adam and Bryce . . . and then maybe she could make an exception.

It seemed to her that Bryce and Adam were always the exception to every rule.

Maybe they can master me. I wonder if they'll ever tie me up again, and then spank me.

The thought itself shocked her. The rational part of her brain said she shouldn't ever think such thoughts.

Kimberly seldom listened to the rational part of her brain, and when she did, she almost always regretted it.

She could feel her climax approaching with each passing second. She sucked Adam's tongue deeper into her mouth, then ended the kiss and looked down at Bryce, who was on his knees on the floor with his arms around her thighs and his mouth busy with her pussy.

"Just a little more," she said to Bryce, her tone taut and hoarse, her orgasm just seconds away. "You . . . you're so good to me . . . when you do that."

She was glad that he didn't stop his pleasuring to respond

to her. She didn't want him saying anything. Though she loved the sound of his voice, she didn't want to hear it just now. All she needed was for him to continue sucking on her clit the way he was, and that was all she would need to be transported into ecstasy.

There's nothing in the world that should feel this right, Kimberly thought. *It's not right.*

But hardly had this thought entered her head than she realized that the entire notion of denying pleasure was not simply foolishness, it was wrong.

He's going to make me come again.

She looked down at Bryce. His face was pressed tightly against her pussy. She could only see him from his nose upward. His eyes were closed, but when they opened, there was a dreaminess in them that pleased her. He was concentrating on pleasuring her. His full concentration was on her ecstasy.

I love that man, she thought, looking at the gorgeous man who was sucking on her clit with a skill and passion that other women would kill to experience.

"Fuck," she said, even though she disliked either to say or hearing the coarse word. "He's going to make me come again."

She turned her gaze from Bryce up to Adam. His eyes were as blue and clear as they always were, but on his face was a smile of sublime serenity.

"Come, darling," Adam said softly, his fingertips grazing lightly over her cheek as he spoke. "He loves the taste of your passion . . . and so do I."

"Fuck," Kimberly said again, though she wished she hadn't.

Then she came. Powerfully. The convulsions were so intense they were nearly painful. And what shocked her most was the number of spasms that went through her during her orgasm. It wasn't just one or two or three times when her body seemed to turn inside out and she was buffeted with waves of pure ecstasy that shook her body.

I mustn't scream.

It was the only conscious thought she had when the tsunami of erotic ecstasy went through her like waves crashing against the shore, each one more powerful than the last.

"Stop . . . please," she said when it seemed to her that the last of the powerful spasms had finally subsided.

She was wrong. Even after Bryce stopped using his lips and tongue with such devastating effect, she climaxed once more.

When the tumult was finally over, she opened her eyes and looked up into Adam's lovely blue eyes and asked, in a soft and utterly sincere tone, "Can we do this again . . . soon? I would be ever so grateful."

CHAPTER THIRTEEN

Inga was nervous, but she was certain everything would work out alright because Caleb had told her that it would, and everything that she had learned during her love life with Caleb was that when he said with certainty that something would happen, then it would happen.

It was all the guarantee in life that she needed.

She looked over her shoulder at Maggie and said softly, "Don't worry. He's thought this through. He always thinks things through. Everything will be okay if we just do what he has planned."

Caleb wasn't a man who left anything up to chance. He just didn't, and that was something that Inga had learned to appreciate . . . and love.

His mind excited her libido more than his body. His glorious body was just as addictive to the erotic mind that she had fallen in love with.

Once again, she thought herself to be the luckiest woman in the world.

"When the cab shows up, get in and then get down. The less people who see us, the better."

She looked down at Maggie. The girl's face was pale, almost ashen. She was frightened. Inga could see that.

"It'll be okay. Just do exactly as I tell you, and soon this will all be over." She cleared her throat and then said, "I promise."

She believed in the hastily concocted plan because Caleb had said it would work. His confidence was all she needed.

They were standing near the front batwing doors to the

Cattleman's Emporium, at the elbow of the man who made sure that nobody could go up the stairs leading to the executive offices. He was an unsmiling man with a gaze that never settled anywhere for long. Inga wondered if he'd been born with suspicious eyes.

Inga heard the sound of horse hooves against the cobblestones outside. The security man looked over the batwing doors, then turned his head and said in a voice that was deep and, frankly, a little scary to hear, "It's here."

She took Maggie's hand. The security man opened the door for them, and they exited quickly onto the boardwalk outside. The hansom cab had its doors already open. Inga recognized the driver's face though she didn't know his name. They'd never been introduced. He was one of the quiet men who always carried a gun and almost never talked. He worked for Caleb.

They stepped up into the cab and the instant the doors closed in front of them, the driver slapped the reins on the horse's back, and they were off.

The horse pulling the cab was nearly at a gallop he was moving so fast. Inga felt her heart rate accelerating. They weren't moving at a speed that was unsafe, but they were very near it. And if they drew attention to themselves, it would be the worst possible outcome.

Caleb has thought this through, she told herself. *Everything will be alright because he's thought this through.*

They turned off the main street and onto a dark side road. The driver slowed, then reined in the horse to a quick stop.

"Here you go, ladies," the driver said. "Off now quickly before anyone notices."

Inga grabbed Maggie's hand and pulled her out of the hansom cab, across the brief space of dirt street, then into the next waiting, enclosed two-horse carriage. Within seconds they were moving rapidly down the dark street with no one the wiser.

"It won't be long now," Inga said quietly. "We'll be in Caleb's arms before you know it."

Caleb was standing on the front porch of his ranch house when they arrived. He seemed, at that moment to Inga, to be impossibly large. He was tall and broad-shouldered and though he wasn't smiling—he seemed much too serious about the things that were happening to be smiling—he was nothing less than gorgeous in Inga's eyes.

I love that man, Inga thought as the coach she was riding in came to a stop. *Almost from the very first moment that I set eyes on him, I have been in love with him.*

The awareness came as something of a shock to her. She knew she was in love with Caleb. She just hadn't realized that she'd *always* been in love with him. Now, suddenly to her, it seemed so perfectly obvious. It seemed rather odd to her that she hadn't understood that simple fact sooner.

Please, please, please let this night be everything that I want it to be.

Inga was aware that she seldom asked wishes from deities—at least not for herself. She often had prayers, but not for something she wanted. But this time, what she wanted was much more important than anything else. This time her heart was invested, it was on the table like a bid that she'd put toward a hand of cards, and she was both thrilled and frightened of what might happen when all the cards were face-up on the table and the highest hand would be there for everyone to see.

"I have a bottle of champagne on ice," Caleb said the instant she stepped out of the carriage.

Very nearly crying with gratitude, Inga asked facetiously, "Just one?"

"There are three, actually," Caleb replied, and now he was smiling. "And strawberries, and whipped cream. Tonight seems to be a night worthy of treats like champagne, strawberries, and whipped cream." In a softer voice he said, "I've also had the cooks ready to make us a feast, in case we work up an appetite."

It took an act of willpower for her to keep herself from throwing herself into Caleb's arms and kissing him with an uninhibited passion that went well beyond mere wantonness.

Inga could feel her clit come alive to the possibilities of ecstasy. It always did whenever she was near Caleb, but tonight it was more prominent in her emotions than at other times. She felt her pussy getting wetter by the second.

Tonight is special, Inga thought. *I don't quite know how or why, but tonight is different from all other nights.*

A shiver went through Inga. She didn't really know what the future held in store for her, but the one thing she was certain of was that she would experience sexual pleasure in the extreme. When she was with Caleb, she always did.

Always.

"No one followed you?" Caleb asked.

"Foolish question," Inga replied without hesitation. "Your men would never allow such a thing."

Caleb nodded.

Inga took Maggie's hand and gave it a firm squeeze. "Let's get inside and pour ourselves some champagne. There's nothing quite like ice cold champagne to ease the nerves."

Inga was only a little surprised to find that there were no servants at hand. Caleb had dismissed them for the night. Even though their loyalty was without question, Caleb would always err on the side of caution. It was the way he was. It was the way his mind always worked.

"Upstairs," Caleb said, taking both Inga and Maggie by the elbow and leading them toward the stairs. "I've got a table set for us. The cooks are ready to make a feast you just won't believe."

Inga said beneath her breath, "I didn't come here for a good supper."

"Let me indulge you. I want you to feel pampered."

I love this man, Inga thought, and though she wanted to tell him so, she did not. Her emotions were so new to her she didn't know how to respond to them. He inspired in her feelings more powerful than what she could fully comprehend.

He understands my lust for him . . . but I'm not so certain he'll understand my love for him.

Inga felt her heart clench at the thought. The importance it had on her life and her happiness could hardly be fathomed.

Don't think about it too much, she told herself. *Too much thinking can only lead to heartache.*

With a certain sense of sadness, she understood that she mustn't let her heart have too much influence over her emotions. It simply wouldn't be wise.

But she was growing very wary of being wise. The more she told herself to be thoughtful, the more she doubted the wisdom of her decisions.

And the more she pondered, the less confident she had in the things she decided. She felt herself to be nothing more than a bundle of uncertainties, and all of them were at war with each other.

When they reached the upstairs room, there was a dining table formally set for them. Caleb referred to it with a casual wave of his hand as he walked purposefully to the wheeled cart that held bottles of liquor, and a large ice bucket that had three bottles of champagne—one of which was already opened.

"I think you'll like this year's vintage," Caleb said as he pulled the bottle out of the ice with a certain theatrical flourish. "It's from a small vineyard in France. They don't usually export, but for me they make exceptions."

Inga watched as he poured a champagne flute full of the bubbly liquor. Looking at the white foam above the golden liquid made her mouth water. She hadn't had properly chilled champagne in more years than she could remember.

"It's good to finally have the two of you here, in my home," Caleb said, his tone infinitely sincere.

Inga felt the urge to kiss him, and though the desire was very strong, she resisted.

"I've wanted to have you here for quite some time, but circumstances just wouldn't allow." He paused a moment before continuing. "I'm sure you understand."

Inga knew that Caleb was trying to protect her reputation. How many women married to much older, wealthy men had been in this ranch house? He made love to them, though he didn't love them. But it wasn't his love they were interested in. It was his skill at amour. And if those women weren't worried about gossip that would surely follow a married woman who had spent the afternoon and much of the evening at Caleb's ranch house, then he wasn't worried about it either.

But with Maggie and herself, he was much more cautious. He didn't take chances with their reputations, no matter how fiery his libido was burning. And for that, Inga adored him. Her feelings for him were much more intense than simple adoration. That word didn't do justice for what she felt.

"I want to show you my home." He smiled charmingly. "I want to show off."

"Later," Inga replied. "In good time."

She took her first sip of the champagne, and it was every bit as delicious as she could have hoped for. She looked at Caleb. When she saw the concern in his eyes regarding her opinion of the champagne, she nodded and smiled reassuringly.

Caleb's in control now, Inga thought with confidence. *Everything will be perfect.*

She watched as Maggie took a very small sip of her champagne. The girl smiled, and when she did, so did Caleb. He was happy just to have given her pleasure.

"This champagne is divine," Inga said to Caleb. She turned

to Maggie and added, "You can have more than a glass or two, darling. You can set yourself free tonight. I'll protect you." She let her tone get softer, more intimate, and added, "I'll always protect you. Caleb and I will always do that."

Inga looked around the room. There was a distinctly masculine flavor to the furnishings. Mostly solid, polished wood. Heavy on knotty pine. Inga realized that this was not simply Caleb's ranch home, this was *his* private room. This is where he felt most at peace, most comfortable. In one corner, near the fireplace, there was a wingback upholstered leather chair. Beside it was a round table of red oak with a kerosene lamp, and beside it, a box of sulfur matches. On the table was a thick, leather-bound book. The pages had gold edges. Inga understood that this book was what Caleb was currently reading, and though she was curious as hell, she did not try to find out what the title was.

"You're sure I can't give you a tour of my home?"

Inga looked at him, and though she knew he wanted to show off his ranch house, she smiled and gave her head a little shake. She could experience the beauty of his abode later. Right now, she wanted champagne and Maggie and Caleb—and nothing else really mattered.

The strawberries were enormous, the largest Inga had ever seen. And they were the most succulent. When she dipped one into the whipped cream, then took a bite of the fruit, she wondered what it would be like to have such delicacies at one's beck and call.

In her world—in the world she had always known—things like strawberries and whipped cream weren't just luxuries, they were impossibilities. But Caleb lived with them every day. Every single day.

"Do you like?" Caleb asked, looking at Inga intently as she chewed the delicious fruit. He was truly concerned with her opinion.

Inga nodded, then rolled her eyes expressively. She could tell that Caleb was trying to impress her, and as flattering as that was, there was a part of her that wanted to explain that he needn't try so hard. There wasn't anything about him that didn't make her think favorably about him. She doubted that, even if he tried, he could make her think anything less than lovingly about him. The more she learned about him, the more she loved him.

Turning to Maggie, Inga asked, "What do you think of the champagne and strawberries?"

Maggie's eyes closed as she chewed, her jaw moving slowly as she savored the fruit in her mouth. "I feel like I've been somehow moved from Montana to Heaven." She turned her gaze from Inga to Caleb, then back again. "Is that even possible? Truly. I feel like I'm in Heaven."

"When you're here, you can think of this as Heaven," Caleb said. There wasn't the slightest bit of uncertainty in his tone. This was a man who believed with all his heart and soul what he'd just said.

The urge, once again for Inga, was to throw herself into his arms. She did not . . . though she promised herself that soon she would. She suspected she owed that to him—and to herself.

Inga watched as Maggie took another strawberry and dipped it into the whipped cream. Though the action itself wasn't overtly or even subtly sexual, to Inga it seemed to be the most erotic actions she'd ever seen a woman—young or experienced—make.

Or would a more appropriate word be *perform?* Inga thought about this a moment before she decided that Maggie's eroticism was without artifice. She was simply being who she was while eating the strawberries, and that was gloriously erotic.

I can't believe she's a part of my life, Inga thought. *I never thought I could get so lucky.*

She turned her gaze toward Caleb and saw that he, too, was paying very careful attention to Maggie as she nibbled on the strawberry.

He's as enchanted with her as I am, Inga thought, feeling herself to be doubly blessed.

Caleb drew attention to himself subtly, then said, "Is there something more that you want? Something you'd like to eat?"

"Yes," Inga said in a firm tone. "You and Maggie."

Caleb was taken aback, but only for a moment before he said, "I can arrange that."

CHAPTER FOURTEEN

Maggie felt as though she was in another world, and the new world she was in was one where limitless pleasure was something that was expected, not something that was only dreamed of but never experienced. Before she had seen the full splendor of Caleb's ranch home, she was in his bedroom, and standing beside the largest bed she'd ever seen. The bedspread was obviously tailor-made, and on it was the symbol of the Cattleman's Emporium, black against the white background.

Maggie wondered what it must be like to have a symbol that everyone sees and understands and recognizes. Everyone in Montana understood what the Ce symbol meant, and they either despised it, revered it, or feared it. But they all understood what it meant, and realized the power behind it, and who and what it represented.

Maggie's lust for Caleb had just gone up several degrees after coming to that awareness, and she felt herself fortunate to be standing within a few feet on the man who controlled such a dynasty.

"Can I kiss you?"

The words seemed to come from a great distance at first, and Maggie did not realize that they were directed at her. Then she looked up into the handsome face of the man who had just spoken those words, and she found herself coming back into her body, into the world that she was living in.

"Yes," she said after an uncomfortably long silence. "You can always kiss me. Whenever and wherever you want." She almost said *I'm yours for the taking* but she did not.

She felt herself blush, since she hadn't intended on being so blunt with Caleb, but the shimmering look of delight she saw in his eyes let her know she'd done nothing wrong.

"A bed," Inga said quietly, running her palms over the surface of the bedspread. "What a luxury. I was afraid that all I'd ever get was the sofa in your office, or the floor."

"I'm sorry for that," Caleb said. "It wasn't the way I wanted it to be . . . but I was concerned about gossip This is a town where people talk, and quite often the things they say can be very cruel."

Maggie looked at him and in that moment she knew that he would always protect her, under any circumstances, no matter what the situation was. He would, she knew at that moment, always be on her side, always defend her against all opposition.

"I love you," she heard herself say. "You know that, right? I mean, you've always known that haven't you?"

Caleb looked down into Maggie's eyes. After several seconds he said, "Yes, I know that. I think I've always known that. But it's nice to hear you say it." He smiled, and the dimple in his cheek came into prominence. "When you first came into my life, I thought you'd be nothing but a nuisance. Now that you're in my life, I can't imagine living without you." He sighed, and his enormous shoulders rose and fell. "There would be no sunshine in my life without you in my world."

"You," Maggie said, struggling to keep her voice steady and her emotions in control, "have way too many clothes on."

"I can change that immediately."

In less than a minute, Maggie, Inga, and Caleb were completely naked, and on Caleb's enormous bed. To Maggie, it felt heavenly to have a mattress beneath her, with soft blankets and a bedspread to caress her naked skin. It was almost more than she had dared to hope for.

"All of my dreams have at last come true," Caleb said, his voice hardly more than a whisper, his tone more honest than anything Maggie had ever heard. The sincerity in his tone nearly made her cry.

Maggie pushed her fingers into his hair, then she leaned forward and inhaled deeply. She loved the smell of him. His scent triggered in her a sexual response that was shockingly powerful, primitive, and most of all, instinctive. It touched her to a level that went beyond the skin, and even deeper than the bone. It touched her soul . . . and it made her tremble with desire. She felt a passion like she'd never had before.

"Kiss me," she whispered. Even *she* could hear the desperation in her tone. "Kiss me like you mean it."

"I couldn't kiss you any other way," Caleb replied, then delivered a kiss that touched Maggie's mouth, and every receptive nerve of sensuality in her body. Especially her clit, which was distinctly ready to receive pleasure that she knew Caleb was more than willing to administer.

For nothing less than thirty seconds Maggie kissed Caleb, delving her tongue deep into his mouth, drinking the heady wine of his desire for her.

Then she turned her face toward Inga. She didn't have long to wait before she was once again being kissed passionately, though this time there was no mustache involved. This time it was nothing more than a woman's soft lips, gentle and sweet and infinitely arousing.

"If ever either of you stop kissing me, I surely will die," Maggie said with a sincerity that only an eighteen-year-old can have.

Inga kissed her again, only this time it was more aggressive, more commanding, and because of it, Maggie felt her pussy clench and become moister.

Quite suddenly, she understood the submissive essence of her passion, and to her complete surprise, she did not just accept it, she embraced it.

Take me, she thought as Inga's tongue explored her mouth. *Take me however you want me. I don't care. With you I know I'm safe. With you I know everything will be alright.*

"Maggie . . . get down on your knees."

It was Caleb who had spoken, and the tone of his voice indicated he would not allow Maggie to in any way resist his command. He was in control now, and to deny that was to risk punishment.

What will he do to me if I defy him?

The thought sent a shiver up and down Maggie's spine. She would never even consider defying Caleb. But the thought of what her punishment might be made her consider refusing his demand. Taboo pleasures of a luscious kind seemed very near, yet slightly out of reach. It was almost as though she could touch them, but not grasp them.

Maggie felt hands on her shoulders, one feminine, one masculine. Both were pushing her down. She resisted at first, but only because she thought it would give the right impression. Then she was on her knees, exactly where she wanted to be. She watched as the woman she loved move into position slightly to her right, and the man she loved moved slightly to her left.

Maggie watched as her fingers curled around the thick, warm shaft of Caleb's incredible cock. When she held him in her hand, she couldn't touch her fingertips to her thumb. He was too thick for that.

For several seconds, she stroked her hand back and forth, feeling the power and virility Caleb possessed, consciously aware that life and luck had been very, very kind to her of late. Perhaps the fates had been cruel to her earlier, but now they were not merely kind, they were generous to the point of being extravagant.

Inga said softly, putting her hips forward toward Maggie slightly, "Don't forget about me." She made a soft sound in her throat and added, "I'm here, too."

Maggie tilted her head back on her shoulders to look up into the woman's face. She saw, then, the uncertainty that Inga felt, and it seemed utterly bizarre to Maggie that Inga would be insecure about anything. Maggie did not say this, though. Instead, she leaned forward and planted a moist, somewhat noisy kiss to Inga's abdomen, just above the triangular pubic hair that grew above her pussy. The hair was slightly darker than the blonde on her head.

Maggie kissed the velvety flesh several times before she inhaled deeply. When she did, she smiled.

"I can smell the scent of your passion," she said without looking up. "You make my mouth water."

As she stroked Caleb's fiercely rigid cock, she began working her tongue between the lips of Inga's pussy, moving slowly and deliberately, starting from the bottom then working her way to the top until she reached Inga's clit. When she was at the small, erect button of flesh, she licked it several times, then captured it between her lips and sucked lightly on it. The moans she elicited from Inga told her everything she needed to know.

She felt Inga stroke her hair, her palm light and comforting, the soft sounds she made in the back of her throat a gentle symphony of serene sensuality.

I could be on my knees in front of her for hours . . . and it wouldn't be long enough to satisfy me.

Maggie opened her eyes and looked up. She saw that Inga's eyes were closed. She was concentrating on the pleasure that Maggie was providing.

Maggie added just a bit more suction on Inga's clit, then released it. She whispered, "I'll be back soon. I promise."

Maggie turned toward Caleb. His cock seemed even bigger than it had been. When she looked at the slit in the crown, she saw an opaque drop of fluid glistening.

He's ready for me, Maggie thought. *This is going to be a long night. A very long time.*

As she took his cockhead into her mouth, Maggie thought herself to be a young woman of almost unfathomable good fortune.

"Deeper," she heard Caleb say. "As deep as you can."

Maggie tried to take his erection into her throat, but she could not. He was much too thick for that. Perhaps if her pathetic Billy had asked the same, she might have been able to. But Caleb was so much more than Billy. More in every conceivable way.

She tongued his slit, and when she did, she tasted the salty drop of pre-come that oozed out. In opposition to what she actually felt, she moaned soulfully and more than a bit theatrically. She wanted Caleb to know without doubt that she thirsted for what he could give her . . . even if she wasn't being entirely honest with him.

Maggie was learning that sometimes a little deception can be good for a relationship.

Briefly, she wondered how many young women had come to this understanding while on their knees.

Maggie tried once again to take Caleb into her throat. When she tried, she choked again and pulled back quickly.

"Stop that," Caleb said sharply. "I don't want you hurting yourself. Not for me. I'm telling you, it's not that important."

Maggie looked up into his face. When she peered into his eyes, she saw the sincerity there. Sincerity . . . and a touch of guilt. At that moment, aware that he felt responsible for her choking in her effort to provide him pleasure and accede to his wishes, she didn't simply love the man—now she flat-out adored him.

Very slowly, with her gaze never once leaving Caleb's, she licked from the base of his shaft all the way up to the underside of the crown. She tongued him there for several seconds, then lewdly pushed her lips over the head of his cock, moaning wantonly, making sure there was no doubt in his mind that she loved being on her knees for him.

"Get up," Caleb said shapely, the glow in his eyes almost frightening to Maggie. "Get on the bed this instant or you'll get a spanking like you've never had in your life."

The thought of getting spanked by Caleb was nearly—very nearly—enough to make her defy his demand.

She had little choice an instant later when he took her arm just above the elbow, turned her to face the enormous bed, then grabbed her by the waist, hoisted her several feet in the air, and threw her face-down on the mattress.

She couldn't keep from laughing as she bounced on the bed.

An instant later he was on her, his chest against her back, his cheek against hers, his weight pressing her into the mattress. His thighs were outside of hers, and his long, fiercely rigid cock was between her legs and pressing hotly against the lips of her pussy.

She felt Caleb's hand in her hair. He clinched it into a fist. Slowly, he pulled her head to the side to expose her neck. Then she felt his lips at her throat. At first he just kissed her, but that didn't last long. A moment later he was nipping at her throat, then sucking hungrily, a feral sound of his marginally civilized desires being released.

Suddenly, Caleb's weight was no longer pressing her to the mattress. Instead, he took her by the hips and lifted her as though she weighed no more than a feather. In an instant she was on her hands and knees with Caleb still behind her.

Maggie, hardly experienced in sexual matters, didn't know exactly what was going to happen next.

She wasn't at all surprised when the inevitable became reality.

"Fuck!" she shouted when she felt the extraordinary girth of Caleb's cock spreading the lips of her pussy. She was slick with excitement, but having Caleb's exquisite erection pushing into her still took some getting used to. "Oh . . . oh . . ." she whispered when he withdrew, and then pressed forward once again.

Maggie was aware that Caleb wasn't ramming everything he had into her immediately. She understood that he was aware of the man that he was, and that under these circumstances a certain sophistication and savoir vivre was necessary.

She felt arms, soft and feminine, slip around her, then hugging her to a velvet-skinned bosom of extravagant dimensions. To feel the side of her face pressing into the twin mounds of Inga's breast was nothing short of heavenly.

Maggie was suddenly and shockingly aware that she had everything in her life that she could ever want or need for her to be happy. The most beautiful, passionate, feminine woman in the world, and the most masculine, handsome man were hers—and they were both making love to her like she was nothing less than a goddess.

She felt Caleb's erection slide deeper into her. At that moment it seemed that there was no limit to how far he could invade. And as she took wonder and glory in Caleb's penetration, she marveled at the velvety softness of Inga's luscious breasts caressing her.

It was when she felt Caleb's pelvis came in contact with her bottom, and the entire lengthy of his manhood was buried inside her silken sheath, that the first spasms of her orgasm began. Her voice was sharp and clear as ecstasy ripped through her in pulsing waves of uninhibited sensuality.

"Give . . . give me a second," she said when the last contraction had at last subsided, and coherent thought was again possible. "I promise I'll do whatever either of you want of me . . . but I need a minute to . . . become human again." She sighed softly, soulfully. "I feel like I owe you both about a dozen climaxes. Are we keeping count? If we are, then I know

I have a great debt to you both."

As Inga gently rubbed her erect nipple against Maggie's cheek, she said, "Darling, pleasing you is all I could ever want."

Chapter Fifteen

Inga took Caleb's cock into her mouth, and she was pleased that she could taste Maggie's juices on him. Though it shocked the hell out of her, she found it wildly erotic to watch the man she loved make love to the girl she loved.

I'm sure I shouldn't feel this way, but I don't care, she thought. *I'm in love with a beautiful man, and he's in love with me. And we're both in love with a girl who delights us in ten thousand different ways.*

"I won't ask if that was good," Inga said, stroking Maggie's hair away from her face as she held her in her lap. "It obviously was."

Maggie whispered, "Caleb's so . . ."

Inga chuckled lightly. She resisted the urge to bring her right nipple to Maggie's mouth. Instead, she said, "I agree. Aren't we lucky that that's so?"

Maggie whispered, "Fuck yes."

Inga replied, "Indelicately but accurately put." She turned her head and looked at Caleb, and in his blue eyes saw a red-hot lust that she was willing to finally set free no matter what the consequences.

"Your cock is mine for the future until I say otherwise," Inga said, her Swedish accent more pronounced with her arousal. "I'm usually not one to make demands, but you've made me greedy. And seeing how calm and satisfied Maggie is, I want to experience the same state of bliss. So, tell me . . . do you think you can fuck me straight into Valhalla?"

"My dearest darling, I will give it my all."

Inga's first climax very nearly caused the crown of her head to come right off. The second wasn't quite as powerful as the first, though it had the benefit of a third orgasm that followed only seconds later.

"Stop!" Inga screamed, though she really didn't mean it, and Caleb knew she didn't want him to, so he kept on with his labors and Inga climaxed one more time. And afterward, when she begged him to stop, he knew she meant it this time, and he did as she requested.

Inga looked at Caleb, then at Maggie. For a moment she wondered how in hell all this had happened, but then she simply closed her eyes.

My world is more blissful than I ever dreamed it would be. Stop thinking and just let yourself feel.

She was almost sleeping when she realized that though he and Maggie had enjoyed multiple climaxes, Caleb—always the gentleman in such matters, it seemed—hadn't had even had a single one.

And Inga knew from experience that one orgasm simply wasn't enough to satisfy the libido of Caleb Essex. He required at least two, and sometimes three or more climaxes before he was truly satisfied.

She turned then and slightly crawled up the bed. She kissed Caleb on the cheek. She heard him sigh and felt the movement of his chest. His arm slipped around her shoulders. She could feel the warmth of his breath in her hair.

"Don't worry about it," he said, reading her mind perfectly. "Everything is fine."

"But . . ."

"Don't worry about it."

"I'm not taking no for an answer," Inga said, and then to emphasize her point, she licked Caleb's left nipple before sucking on it.

His low groan was music to Inga. Her palm was on his stomach. She pushed it lower, felt the crinkly hair above his manhood, then wrapped her fingers around the cock that had taught her what real ecstasy really was.

"This has got to be taken care of or your chef will never get the chance to cook all those culinary delights you promised." Her cheek was against his chest when she felt him chuckle. "Besides, when you asked me what I wanted to eat, I did include you on the menu."

"Hold that thought," Caleb said, taking Inga by the wrist and easing her hand off his cock. "There's something I have to do first."

With athletic grace and seemingly unmindful that there might be any servants in the other room, Caleb rolled out of bed and strode out of the room.

Rolling toward Maggie, Inga watched the girl yawn, then stretch, then blink her eyes several times.

"I'm afraid I'm falling asleep. He's worn me out." She yawned again. "But I have to stay awake. Caleb's not ready to call it a night, and he'll want me to help you satisfy him."

"I can take care of him. Just close your eyes and get some sleep." Inga chuckled. "Don't worry, Caleb will want us both again in the morning."

A short while later Caleb returned. His erection had diminished, but it hadn't gone down completely. When he entered the room, he stopped and just looked at Inga and Maggie as though in mystified wonder.

Inga rolled slightly so that he had a full view of the front of her body. She knew from experience that he found the size, shape, and firmness of her breasts to be of significant interest.

"Why don't you pour yourself a whiskey and come and relax. Just let me take care of everything." Inga combed her fingers through her long blonde hair to get it away from her face. Caleb liked to watch her when she pleasured him with her mouth, and she liked to be watched. "I know just exactly how to put a satisfied smile on your face."

She watched as Caleb crossed the room to the chest-of-drawers where, on its tabletop, was a bottle of his finest whiskey, and a cut crystal lowball glass. Caleb had clearly planned in advance for what was about to happen. Watching him walk, he seemed to her like a powerful lion in his absolute prime with an enormous pride of lionesses to satisfy.

He filled his glass and started toward the bed, but Inga sat up and gave her head a little shake.

"In a bit you can sit and lean back against the headboard to enjoy me and your whiskey," Inga said, easing off the bed and sinking to her knees. "To begin with I want you standing in front of me. When I'm on my knees and you're standing, in my eyes you're a giant." She cupped her breasts, immediately capturing the nipples between her forefingers and thumbs. She pinched her nipples, and with the other three fingers of each hand, she squeezed and caressed her breasts. Caleb's cock wasn't yet in her mouth before the warm, enticing tingles from her self-administered caresses began working their way throughout her body.

She opened her lips as Caleb guided the bulbous crown between them. A soft, sensuous moan came from her as she tightened her lips around the shaft, just behind the cockhead. She tugged and twisted just a little more firmly on her breasts, and the throbbing warmth it caused went straight to her clit.

Her eyes had drifted closed, but now she opened them so that she could look up into Caleb's eyes. She watched as he took a sip of his cocktail. In his eyes was a look of unfathomable delight. He seemed to be a hundred feet tall. With his free hand he smoothed a lock of honey-blonde hair behind her ear, then caressed her temple with a touch as delicate as a butterfly's wings.

"So beautiful," Caleb said, a certain growl in his voice now that his lust was once again racing. His formidable erection was growing to its full dimensions as he moved his hips slowly back and forth to slide the head and shaft of his cock between Inga's lips and over her tongue. "I like it when I look down at you and see that you're on your knees. It makes me feel like I'm a king. It makes me understand just how much good fortune I've had in my life . . . but none of it compares to what I've had with you." He smiled a bit crookedly. "Well, you and Maggie."

Caleb took another manly swallow of his cocktail, then inhaled deeply and sighed. For a moment he closed his eyes in pleasure. The expression on his face was everything and more that Inga could have hoped for.

If he wants me on my knees at the Cattleman's Emporium Saloon with two dozen cowboys surrounding us, watching me, I'll do it.

The thought brought a fission of exhibitionistic lust surging through her veins, and this both shocked and delighted Inga. She sucked just a little more hungrily on Caleb's arousal and pinched and tugged on her sensitive nipples with greater urgency.

Inga heard the bed move, then Maggie said, "Don't you want me to help you with that?"

Inga considered being selfish for a moment, but it was only for a moment. She leaned away from Caleb. He slipped out from between her lips.

"I thought you were sleeping," Inga said, looking over her shoulder at Maggie. She felt more than just a little bit selfish.

"I was sleeping. You should have woken me." There was the petulance of a teenager in her tone that would no longer be there a couple years from this evening. "Did I miss much? I shouldn't have let myself fall asleep."

Inga patted the floor beside her knee. "Come down here with me and we'll share him. He's big enough for the two of us."

Maggie settled on her knees, her hip touching Inga's. The pettish expression she'd had on her face a moment earlier transformed into one of quiet delight as she looked at the long, slick-with-saliva cock that Inga was stroking.

"Go ahead, darling," Inga said as, with her free hand, she stroked Maggie's hair away from her face. Inga didn't want any obstructions to what she was about to see. "You know how to do it. I know that because I was the one who taught you."

A shiver of voyeuristic lust went through Inga when she watched the knob of Caleb's erection slide between the girl's lips and fill her mouth. Maggie raised her hand and tried to wrap it around the shaft, but Inga touched her to indicate she herself would take care of that task. Maggie made a soft, mewling sound in her throat, but otherwise didn't protest. She put her palms down on her thighs.

Inga told herself to not be selfish, but it seemed that Maggie wasn't going to relinquish Caleb without having to be told to—so Inga simply pulled him out of her mouth, then captured him with her own.

"That's enough," Caleb said after several minutes of Inga and Maggie playing tug-of-war with his cock. "Both of you, get on the bed."

The sternness in his tone was all for show, and Inga knew it.

Caleb manhandled them into place, putting Inga on her back in the middle of the bed, and then positioning Maggie so that she straddled Inga's head with her knees.

Oh, yes, Caleb knows what he'd doing, Inga thought as she wrapped her arms around the girl's thighs, then pulled her down to taste the lips of a scrumptious young pussy.

Inga felt Caleb's fiery erection push between the lips of her pussy at exactly the same time she slipped her tongue between Maggie's pink sex lips.

The trio started moving clumsily at first, but then they quickly realized the best way to accomplish their shared objective and began moving in unison. Soon Inga was rocking on the bed as Caleb moved forward and back with controlled strength. Inga held tightly onto Maggie's thighs so that she could keep her mouth against a vagina that seemed to be getting wetter and more delicious by the second.

Inga was thinking that she was handling the whole thing pretty calmly . . . right up to the time Caleb started using his thumb against her clit while he worked his cock full-length in and out of her vagina.

That was when what was happening went from being hot to being a blazing inferno. Inga tightened her arms around the girl's slender thighs even more severely, and she tongued Maggie's clit and sex lips with nothing less than avaricious greed.

The thumb. The seesawing cock. The slender, twitching hips. The nectar that oozed out of Maggie's opening as her excitement grew. The feel of firm, young thighs beneath her hands . . . .

Inga's entire body shook and trembled as she climaxed. Somewhere shortly after her orgasm began, Maggie reached the summit. Inga felt her cheeks getting wet and the honey of the girl's climax dribbling down the sides of her face.

And then there was that leonine roar of masculine ecstasy a split second before Inga no longer had a man deep, deep inside her. She felt the warmth and creaminess of Caleb's come hitting her. She heard Maggie gasp and suspected that she, too, had been splashed by Caleb's sperm. It didn't surprise her. His climaxes were explosive.

What a wonderful mess he's made.

I wouldn't change a single thing.

Inga drifted awake, and though she was only half-conscious, she felt the eerie sense that she was being watched. It concerned her without alarming her.

She blinked her eyes several times to clear her vision. When she could finally see properly in the dim light emanating from the single kerosene lamp in the room that was lit, she saw Caleb. He was wearing a silk robe now. It was black, and because it was, it made only Caleb's face and hands entirely visible in the lamplight. He was holding a glass in his hand. When Inga looked at the bottle of liquor beside him, she saw that much more of it was missing since she had gone to sleep.

He was looking at us as we slept. Since making love, he's been looking at us . . . and brooding about something.

Inga felt a chill go through her.

She smiled sleepily and combed her fingers through her hair. "Come to bed, darling. Come to bed and let me hold you while you sleep. Or you can hold me. You don't need to finish your drink. Whatever comfort you need, I can provide."

"No."

The single word had come out coldly, and with a firmness that indicated he would not change his mind, or even tolerate someone trying to alter his attitude. He was a determined man, and Inga's sense of emotional unease began rising.

She put the blanket aside and got out of bed, getting to her feet but not stepping closer to Caleb—though that's exactly what she wanted to do.

She felt that everything would be better if she could only touch Caleb. But the aura that emanated from him told her that touching him, or even getting close to him, was the last thing that he would allow.

"This isn't right." Caleb made it a declarative sense that couldn't be challenged. "What the three of us are doing, and how we're doing it . . . it isn't right, and we all know it."

Inga whispered to herself, "Oh, God . . . tell me this isn't happening . . ."

"I'm not happy," Caleb continued. "I don't think that any of the three of us are truly happy with the way things are."

In a very soft voice, Inga said, "I'm happy."

"We can't go on like this," Caleb said, his voice rising.

"None of us can be happy. Not the way things are right now."

Inga put a hand to her mouth, and through her fingers she whispered, "I'm happy."

Sharply, Caleb looked her straight in the eyes and said, "I'm not!"

"I am." It was a plea for sympathy.

"I'm not, and because I'm not, things are going to change." He took a big swallow of his whiskey and said, "Don't you see? It's just not right. We can't go on this way."

Inga fell straight down, like a puppet whose strings and just been cut.

With her eyes closed and her hands to her face, she whispered. "I should have known this would happen. I was too happy. It was all too good to be true. It couldn't last because it was all just too good to be true."

EPILOGUE

"The bride looks positively radiant," Adam said, standing at the edge of the dance floor.

Looking at Inga in her white bridal gown as she danced the first dance with her new husband, Caleb, Kimberly replied, "I've never seen her look so happy."

For the first dance of the reception, which had begun immediately after the wedding ceremony, the bride and groom had the dance floor to themselves while the twelve-piece orchestra that had been brought in played a lovely, slow waltz that fit the mood of the moment.

"Rumors are flying," Bryce said between significant sips of the punch, which had been liberally fortified with rum. "Since the gap between the engagement announcement and the wedding was only two weeks, everyone thinks that Inga is pregnant." He chuckled. "Everyone."

"What do you think?" Kimberly asked, keeping her voice low. She was standing at the edge of the dance floor, in her bridesmaid dress, and there were too many people too close for her to speak in a conversational tone.

"I think she is," Bryce replied. "They also think that Maggie is the love child they've kept secret all these years. But what I don't understand is why they're taking Maggie with them on their honeymoon. I can understand them having her move in with them, but—"

"I can explain that," Kimberly said, cutting her lover off quickly. "Left on her own, Maggie makes bad decisions. Inga has really taken her under her wing to protect her, and I suppose she just doesn't want to leave the girl alone and vulnerable to making mistakes for the entire month Caleb and Inga are on their honeymoon."

"I can see Maggie moving into the ranch house with them, but going with them on their honeymoon? I'll bet Caleb's pissed as hell about that. What man would want extra baggage with him on his honeymoon?"

Kimberly raised her eyebrows. "Who the hell knows? All I'm certain of is that Inga right now looks about as happy as a bride can be, and Caleb is beaming with joy. Apparently, the extra baggage isn't dampening the spirit of their honeymoon."

Simultaneously, Adam and Bryce replied, "I just don't get it."

The End

About the Author

Robin Gideon is the author of over 50 novels and novellas in paperback form and for e-publishers. She is currently writing erotic action-adventure stories starring the secret agent Svetlana Simonov exclusively for Extasy Books. She was the featured author on the nationally syndicated TV series CBS Sunday Morning. She loves hearing from her readers, and can be reached at: robin.gideon@ymail.com.

www.ingramcontent.com/pod-product-compliance
Lightning Source LLC
LaVergne TN
LVHW010106170826
845678LV00012B/2259

* 9 7 8 1 4 8 7 4 3 9 3 7 8 *